Ashley's ꞏꞏꞏꞏꞏꞏ dangerous secret . . .

"You can't tell anybody what I'm about to say," Ashley told Christina urgently. "Promise."

"I promise."

"I gave the cat in Dr. Jeffers's office the angelbloom tea and she almost died. She might still die if Dr. Jeffers can't save her."

Shocked, Christina covered her gaping mouth with one hand.

Ashley hated the look on Christina's face, so stunned and horrified. "I thought it was safe," she added in a small voice.

"Ashley, you've got to tell Dr. Jeffers," Christina cried. "If she knows what you've done, maybe she can find a cure."

"I can't tell her," Ashley insisted, turning away. She wasn't a liar. But this was worse than anything she'd ever had to deal with before. She couldn't do the right thing. The right thing was too hard.

The Blossom Angel

FOREVER ANGELS

The Blossom Angel

Suzanne Weyn

Troll

Text copyright © 1996 by Chardiet Unlimited, Inc., and Suzanne Weyn.
Cover illustration copyright © 1996 by Mark English.
Cover border photography by Katrina.
Angel stickers (GS7) copyright © 1991 by Gallery Graphics, Inc., Noel, MO, 64854. Used with permission.

Published by Troll Communications L.L.C.

Printed in the United States of America.

10 9 8 7 6 5 4 3 2 1

For Melissa Weyn, with love

1

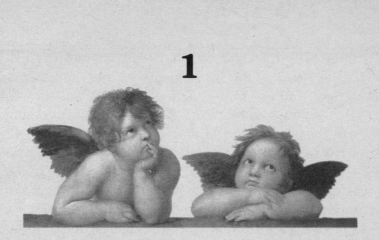

"It's coming. Oh, my gosh. I see it. Here it comes!" Ashley cried. She knelt next to Bridey, the deep brown mare lying on her side on a thick bed of straw. Bridey looked up at Ashley with calm, weary eyes. She snorted, her nostrils quivering as she strained to bring her foal into the world.

Ashley mopped the horse's sweaty side with a cool, damp cloth.

"Steady, girl, steady," soothed Dr. Jeffers, the veterinarian who knelt on the other side of Bridey. With the back of her hand, she quickly brushed the bangs of her short gray hair from her intense dark eyes, then leaned forward, stroking Bridey's stomach with strong, confident hands. "You're almost done," she said to the trembling, sweating mare. "Hang in there."

Suddenly the shiny wet black head of a foal emerged from Bridey's body. Bridey whinnied sharply and whipped the hay with her tail.

"Come on, girl, come on," Dr. Jeffers urged.

Ashley blew a strand of long, curly orangish-red hair from her eyes. She looked up at her tall, broad-shouldered father leaning against the wall of the stall. Their eyes met, and he nodded to her with a tired smile. Though his eyes were red with sleeplessness—knowing Bridey was about to give birth, he'd slept in the barn—they were also filled with quiet emotion. He'd been hovering close by, assisting where he could, ever since Dr. Jeffers had arrived at five-thirty this morning.

Ashley's eyes misted with tears. The birth of this foal was one of the most moving events she'd ever witnessed. She felt as though she were at the center of one of life's greatest mysteries, as if she were at the center of life itself.

"All right! All right!" she cheered, a throb of happiness in her voice, as the foal slid into Dr. Jeffers's waiting arms. "You did it, Bridey! Way to go!"

"It's a filly," Dr. Jeffers announced, smiling, "a little girl!"

The exhausted mare whinnied softly while Dr. Jeffers finished up with the birth. Dr. Jeffers nodded at the filly. "She's a beauty, isn't she?"

"She sure is," Ashley said. "Beautiful."

Dr. Jeffers got to her feet and peeled off her rubber gloves. "She looks fine to me," she told Mr. Kingsley. "I'll examine her fully a bit later. What are you naming her?"

"I'll let Ashley do that," he replied.

Dr. Jeffers smiled, and her delicate, finely lined face appeared younger than her sixty-three years. "Ashley's a natural with horses. I can see that," she said, as Bridey hauled herself to her feet with deep huffing breaths.

"She's good with all animals," Mr. Kingsley added, his

eyes on the new filly. "When our dog, Champ, was a puppy, she was the only one who could get him to mind, even though she was only four herself."

No one spoke as the filly flailed her long legs until she finally struggled onto her spindly knees. From there, she pushed back and straightened her hind legs. "Should we help her up?" Ashley asked as the little horse rocked back and forth, seemingly stuck in that position.

"No," Dr. Jeffers said. "Let her do it herself."

"Does that matter?" Ashley inquired.

"I'm not sure that it does," Dr. Jeffers replied, "but I'm not sure that it doesn't, either. And, since I don't know, I think it's best to let nature take its course. There's no rush. She'll get there."

As Bridey licked her wet child, the filly gazed up at her with impossibly huge and liquid eyes. For a moment, Ashley thought the newborn was content enough to doze off in her awkward position, but then she started rocking again. Ashley gasped each time the unsteady foal seemed about to totter and fall. But after several attempts, she rocked her front half up to match her back half. She was up on all fours.

Ashley clapped with delight as the filly found her footing. Bridey licked her thoroughly, and then the filly nuzzled determinedly at her mother's belly.

"We can let mother and baby alone now," Dr. Jeffers said, taking her faded khaki-green barn jacket from where she'd draped it over the stall.

"Want some coffee and breakfast?" Mr. Kingsley offered.

"Sounds good," Dr. Jeffers replied, smiling.

Yawning widely, Ashley followed them past the other

horses. On her way out, she stopped to look at Champ. The family's golden retriever lay sleeping on his cozy red-flannel dog bed in his favorite spot, the sunny corner closest to the stable door.

As if he could feel her gaze upon him, Champ groggily opened his gold-flecked brown eyes and lifted his head. Bending, Ashley rubbed the soft fur between his floppy ears. "Sorry to wake you, pal," she said. "We had a girl."

Blinking twice, Champ adjusted his position and settled back to sleep, his head resting on his paws.

Outside the stable, Ashley squinted at the gentle dawn light. She'd been so excited about the prospect of Bridey's impending birth, she'd slept on the living room couch completely dressed. She'd awakened in the dark to hear her father calling Dr. Jeffers on the kitchen phone. Like lightning, Ashley had swung herself off the couch, fully alert.

But now her eyes burned as if filled with sand. Sleep was calling her back.

She spotted her father and Dr. Jeffers several paces ahead. They were crossing the wide path that separated the stable from the neat, light yellow ranch house with its trim white shutters and open front porch. Ashley hurried to catch up with them.

"Was that your first birth?" Dr. Jeffers asked when Ashley came alongside her.

Ashley nodded.

"What did you think?"

"Awesome," Ashley answered.

Dr. Jeffers chuckled. "That's the best word I can think of to describe it. Now that it's spring, I'm not getting much sleep. Every ranch around here has at least two pregnant mares this year."

"Daisy will be the next mare to deliver here," Mr. Kingsley said.

"She's got some time yet," Dr. Jeffers said thoughtfully. "I don't think she'll go until mid-July."

"Do the births always happen at night?" Ashley asked, stifling another yawn.

Dr. Jeffers smiled. "I'm afraid so. Usually at night or early in the morning, like this one."

"How come?" Ashley asked.

"I don't know," Dr. Jeffers admitted, shaking her head. "It's just nature's way."

"But people are born at all different times," Ashley said.

Dr. Jeffers shrugged as they stepped up onto the porch. "Horses aren't people."

"You're lucky," Ashley said. "It must be great to work with animals the way you do."

"I do love it," Dr. Jeffers said. "I wouldn't call it luck, though. It took a lot of hard work to finish school and then keep the practice going."

"It paid off, though," Mr. Kingsley said. "Ask any rancher or farmer in Pine Ridge—you're the only vet they'll let near their animals."

Dr. Jeffers smiled. "I'm not sure that's exactly true," she said, laughing, "but it's nice of you to say so. Are you interested in working with animals, Ashley?"

"I guess I'll always work with horses," Ashley said. "I mean, that's what my whole family has always done. But when I watch you, it makes me think about being a veterinarian. The idea has been in my head lately."

"Really?" Mr. Kingsley said as he pulled open the front door. "I never knew that."

Ashley shrugged, a little embarrassed. "It's a new idea I've had, just lately. I don't know if I'd be able to really do it, but I've been thinking about it."

They went inside and crossed the neat, silent, dawn-lit living room. Mrs. Kingsley still slept, as did Jeremy and Jason, the seventeen-year-old twins. In the cheerful yellow kitchen, Mr. Kingsley began making coffee.

Dr. Jeffers stopped and turned to Ashley with a decisive expression. "I just had a thought, Ashley. I could really use someone to help me out in my practice. Spring and summer are so busy for me, and I'm on the road a lot. Would you be interested in working for me a few hours a week?" She glanced over at Mr. Kingsley. "Of course it would have to be all right with you, Hank."

Mr. Kingsley scratched his bristly unshaven cheek thoughtfully. "I just need Ashley for trail rides and to work over at the bunkhouse once guests start coming in," he said musingly.

Impulsively, Ashley grabbed his wrist. "Please, Dad, please," she pleaded. "I'll do all my chores here. I'll get up super early. Please."

Mr. Kingsley studied Ashley's bright green eyes and pretty, lightly freckled face. "All right," he agreed. "I guess it will be all right."

Tired as she was, Ashley felt a surge of new energy rush through her. "This is so cool!" she said to Dr. Jeffers. "When do I start?"

"How about just on Saturdays until school ends?" Dr. Jeffers suggested. "You can start next Saturday."

"Okay, sure," Ashley said happily. What a great chance! Ashley couldn't think of anything more interesting or fun.

"Good, then it's settled. I can really use you, and you really do have a wonderful way with animals," Dr. Jeffers said, taking a seat at the kitchen table. "By the way, how does Junior seem these days? Still doing well?"

"Better than ever before," Mr. Kingsley answered. "He's turned into one frisky little colt."

Ashley pulled open the refrigerator door and took out a carton of eggs. "It's true," she said, nodding. Junior was a palomino colt, soon to be a yearling. A while ago, he'd been terribly sick. Not even Dr. Jeffers knew how to cure him. Then he'd eaten some flowers Ashley had picked in the woods just behind the ranch. Somehow the flowers had been just what Junior needed to get well.

With Ashley's help, Dr. Jeffers had found the flower listed in one of her old herbal healing books. It was called angelbloom, and once Ashley learned its name, she stopped being surprised at Junior's miracle cure. According to the book, the flower grew only in the mountains of Tibet. Ashley thought she had a pretty good idea of how it mysteriously came to be growing in the Pine Manor woods, just when Junior needed it.

"I'd like to study that angelbloom someday," Dr. Jeffers told Ashley now. "Since it's spring, it might be blooming again. Have you been out in the woods lately, Ashley? Have you seen it?"

"We take trail rides into the woods every day, but I haven't noticed any. I haven't really looked for it, though," Ashley said.

"When you get a chance, could you take a look around for it?" Dr. Jeffers asked as Mr. Kingsley handed her a steaming mug of coffee. "I'd really like to study it, maybe even run some tests on it. It's so strange to find it growing in the Pine Manor woods when my book says it only grows in the freezing mountains of Tibet."

"That *is* odd," Mr. Kingsley murmured as he cracked eggs into a bowl.

Ashley opened a container of orange juice. *It's odder than you can imagine, Dad*, she thought.

There was a secret about the angelbloom that they'd never believe.

And Ashley wasn't about to risk telling them, either.

2

"**O**h, how darling," Christina crooned, excitedly squeezing Ashley's arm as she crept into the stall where Bridey stood beside her foal. After a short nap, Ashley had raced over to tell her friend about the new filly.

"She is *too* cute," Christina trilled adoringly, edging her tall frame cautiously closer. Ashley smiled as her friend cupped the filly's sweet, big-eyed face in her hands. A blissful delight lit Christina's startlingly blue eyes. "You are so-o-o cute," she cooed to the little horse. "Little Baby Bridey." She straightened and patted Bridey. "Good work, Mama. You did good."

"She did, too," Ashley agreed. "I never expected her to be so calm. She's usually such a pain."

Christina frowned, causing the small white scar over her left eyebrow to crinkle. "No she isn't. She's just got spirit. I wish I'd been here to see it. It must have been so exciting."

"You can help when Daisy has her foal," Ashley suggested.

Christina's mother, Alice, worked at the ranch as a stable hand, riding instructor, and trail guide. The small, cozy cabin she and Christina shared was right there on the ranch, just off the dirt road that ran from the entrance all the way to the bunkhouse behind the stable.

Christina twisted her long, corn-colored hair into a knot on top of her head, then deftly fixed it in place with a scrunchy taken from her jeans pocket. "I'd like to be there," she said. "But I wish I'd seen this birth."

Ashley understood. Bridey was Christina's favorite horse. Although skittish, even sometimes nasty, with other people, Bridey settled down almost magically for Christina.

"This filly is a Gemini," Christina said. "She's on the cusp of Taurus, but she's definitely born under Gemini." Christina was deeply interested in astrology and all kinds of other New Age stuff. She'd taught herself to read tarot cards and was working on the Chinese fortune telling system of I Ching and the Native American Indian system of medicine cards. She knew numerology and believed in healing with crystals, among other things.

"What's a cusp?" Ashley asked.

"It means she was born just as the moon was shifting from Taurus into Gemini. People born at those times can show characteristics of both signs."

"Do you think animals are affected by astrology?" Ashley asked, raising a skeptical eyebrow. She herself wasn't sure what she thought of astrology or any of Christina's other spiritual passions. When she was away from Christina, Ashley mostly thought it was all nonsense. But, somehow, when she was with Christina it was easy to believe just the opposite. Christina made it all sound very convincing.

"Why shouldn't it affect them?" Christina countered. "Animals all have their own personalities. Bridey is prickly with most people, while Daisy is calm and sweet. Look at how different Junior is from the other colts. The rest of them are so wild, they can't bear to stand still. And he's just this shy little sweetheart who never wants to leave his mother."

"He's friskier, lately, though. Don't you think?" Ashley said. "I noticed he's been leaving May more and more to go with the other colts."

Christina nodded thoughtfully. "I know what you mean. After he ate the angelbloom, he seemed even stronger than he did before he got sick."

"Dr. Jeffers asked me to look for more angelbloom," Ashley told her. "She wants to run tests on it."

Christina's usually sunny expression darkened with worry. "Does she know how it got into the woods?"

Ashley glanced down at her hands and picked at her chipped nail polish. Ashley always kept her hands perfectly manicured, just as she was careful about her appearance in general. It was important to her that her hair, clothing, jewelry, and even the light makeup she occasionally wore were just so. But today the polish had chipped during her hours in the stable with Bridey. Now that she noticed it, it bothered her.

"Did you tell her about the angelbloom?" Christina repeated.

Ashley looked up from her hands. "I was just thinking about how to answer that question," she said. "I did try to tell her once, half-kidding, when Junior got better after eating the flowers, but she just blew it off. Now I don't want to tell her."

"Why not?" Christina challenged her.

"Well, you know, she offered me a job," Ashley said slowly. "My first real job."

"Yeah?" Christina said.

"I really want it to work out. I don't want her to think I'm nutty or anything like that," Ashley said self-consciously. "Anyway, we don't know for sure about the angelbloom. I'm pretty sure, though, Dr. Jeffers wouldn't believe me if I told her what we think."

"I know what you mean," Christina said, folding her arms. "It's amazing how many people don't want to believe in angels. My own mother doesn't believe we saw them. *My* mother! Of all people!" Alice Kramer was like Christina in her interest in all kinds of unusual things. It was probably where Christina got it from. Alice was open-minded about everything—crystal power, herbal healing, the mystical sciences of ancient cultures, everything—except angels.

Yet, they *had* seen them. Ashley, Christina, and their friends Katie and Molly had all encountered angels deep in the thick Pine Manor woods. It was there at the old Angels Crossing Bridge that the angels appeared, and it was there the girls went when they needed them.

"Maybe it's one of those things you just have to see to believe," Ashley said philosophically.

"Hmphh," Christina huffed.

Bridey whinnied and flicked her full, chestnut tail at them. The girls could see the filly insistently nuzzling at

Bridey. "Maybe mom and baby need some time alone," Christina said. "Let's go."

They left, shutting the stall door behind them.

"Want to go look for more angelbloom?" Ashley asked.

"Sure. Why not? We haven't been to the bridge in a while. I'd like to go."

As soon as they stepped outside the stable, a man and woman in a red sports car stopped on the dirt road in front of them. The woman rolled down the window. "Excuse me," she began. "Can you tell us where we might find the Pine Manor Inn?"

Ashley pointed to a rambling brown building nestled among the pines, a ways down the dirt road. "It's right there. Just park in front." This was the first Saturday they'd opened the bunkhouse for guests since closing for the winter. Ashley was glad to see they had boarders already. Since the inn opened last year, its steady stream of paying guests had helped the ranch's troubled finances a lot.

"Thanks," the woman said as the car pulled away.

Ashley felt something wet on her hand, looked down, and laughed. "Hi, Champ," she said to the affectionate dog who licked her happily.

Champ followed Ashley and Christina around to the back of the stable. They stood a moment, gazing at the rustling pines. Although the evergreens never lost their needles, springtime seemed to have brought with it an extra lushness, a thickening of the pines and the damp foliage running rampant on the ground beneath.

Breathing deeply, Ashley took in the rich, heady smell of pine. For her, the pine smell had become a signal that she was entering a different world—an ancient and magical place.

Christina said it was a special place, full of power spots, places where good energy pooled and swirled like the eddies of a river. Certainly, she said, the Angels Crossing Bridge was a major power spot.

Ashley picked up a stick and hurled it into the woods. With a cheerful bark, Champ lunged after it. "Come on," she said to Christina. "Let's go."

The crunch of footsteps made both Ashley and Christina turn at the same time. In the next second, a tall girl with shoulder-length auburn hair came around the side of the stable, a baseball cap turned brim backward on her head. "There you are," Katie Nelson said. "What's happening?"

"Hi." Ashley greeted their friend. "Why are you here so early?"

"I start working at the inn today, remember?" she said. Katie worked at the inn during the summer doing housekeeping and odd jobs. "Your mom asked if I could work Saturdays and Sundays until school ends. But I'm way early. I had to take a ride with Uncle Jeff this morning or I wouldn't have been able to get here at all. What are you doing?"

"Going to the bridge," Christina explained.

"Cool," Katie said. "Let's go."

As they stepped into the quiet woods, they met Champ returning with the stick in his mouth. "Good boy," Ashley said, laughing and taking it from him. She threw the stick, and again Champ charged after it. "He's still fast for an old dog," she remarked proudly.

The girls made their way deeper into the woods, not really talking, with Ashley tossing the stick for Champ again and again. They traveled over rocky inclines, hopped over fallen trees, and scrambled up mossy embankments. After about ten minutes, they stopped to gaze at a cluster of lacy purple wildflowers whose slender blossoms leaned toward the shard of sunlight that had somehow found its way through the thick canopy of pine branches.

"That's not angelbloom, is it?" Christina wanted to know.

"No," Ashley said, tossing the stick through a narrow space between the pines, whose trunks grew closer together as they went deeper into the woods. "Angelbloom looks more like heather."

"How come we're looking for angelbloom?" Katie asked.

Ashley told her about Dr. Jeffers's offer and how she wanted to study the flower.

"That is so cool," Katie responded. "I think Dr. Jeffers is great. I mean, she's so old, but she doesn't act it at all."

"I know what you mean," Ashley agreed, taking the stick from Champ. "I'm super-excited about working with her. My first real job!"

After a while, the woods grew too dense for Ashley to throw the stick anymore without hitting a tree. Champ sensed the change and stopped frisking. He walked quietly alongside the girls, panting, his long pink tongue hanging as the air became cooler and more richly scented. Beneath their feet, the thick carpet of fallen pine needles muffled their footsteps as they padded silently along.

Above them, a heavy branch groaned. A twig snapped somewhere in the distance. Two squirrels scrambled up a tree, scratching their way along the bark. A bird call sounded exotic and strange. Yet, despite these sounds, Ashley felt she was in the midst of a vast, deep silence, and something inside her grew silent with it.

Her breathing slowed, maybe even her heartbeat. Her thoughts grew less scattered, calmer. She began daydreaming about the new foal, wondering what to name her. Maybe she'd call her Angel.

Eventually the quiet was broken by the welcome, happy sound of burbling, rushing water. The sound assured them they were going in the right direction. It was too easy to get lost in these woods. They followed the water sound to a narrow, rollicking stream that danced over the rocks and branches in its winding path.

The girls followed the stream, Champ merrily splashing through it, until a ways later the stream disappeared, seeming to flow right into the side of a steep hill. They climbed the hill and stopped at its crest. Looking down, they peered at the old covered bridge spanning the wide, rushing creek. Whatever road had ever led to or from the bridge had long since been overgrown with pines. Its roof completely covered the bridge, but sturdy wooden posts supporting the roof left the sides half open, so that the girls could see anything on the bridge and even beyond it.

"I don't see them," Christina noted.

"Me, neither," Ashley replied. She knew Christina was talking about the angels.

Picking up speed as they went, Ashley, Katie, and

Christina headed down the hill, with Champ running ahead. His nails clattered on the wooden boards as he raced onto the bridge, the first to reach it. The girls followed him to the middle of the bridge, their sneakered feet occasionally causing a weak board to groan. They paused a moment, gazing out at the wide creek as it rushed, foaming around boulders.

Christina's hand on her shoulder made Ashley turn. "What?"

"Look over there," Christina told her.

"Oh, my gosh!" Katie murmured.

3

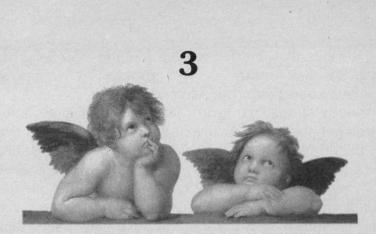

Standing up to their waists in the creek off to the left of the bridge were two women and a man.

They faced one another in a ragged circle and seemed to be looking at something that caused them to clap and laugh with delight.

"*What* are they doing? No, wait, what are they *wearing*?" Ashley asked, leaning over the side of the bridge to get a better look. The outfits were odd, yet somehow familiar, as if Ashley had seen them in an old movie or something.

One of the women wore her long black hair in a single braid. Her old-fashioned white sailor-style bathing suit was cut at sharp angles like the bones of her handsome face.

In contrast, the gorgeous woman next to her wore a ruffled, old-time swimming dress of pink and yellow stripes and a matching bow in the coils of her wavy blonde hair. The man wore a striped one-piece outfit that reminded Ashley of the movie *Chitty, Chitty, Bang, Bang*. His sandy hair was combed straight back off his broad forehead.

"It looks like they're wearing bathing suits from the turn of the century or something. I don't know," Christina observed. "But why?"

Ashley shook her head. She and her friends knew these people. Ned, Edwina, and Norma were often here by the bridge. And they were often doing something odd.

Only they weren't actually people. They were angels.

True, Ned, Edwina, and Norma could be kind of cagey about their real natures. But Ashley knew they were angels. And so did Katie and Christina. They'd seen them in their glorious shining angel forms, with their flowing silvery white gowns and amazing iridescent wings. There could be no doubt about it. Even the usually skeptical Katie couldn't deny the truth of what they'd seen. Ashley and Christina had never even tried.

Christina hurried off the bridge and down the embankment toward the creek. "Hi," she called as she neared the water's edge. More slowly, Ashley and Katie followed with Champ at their heels.

Ned looked up and smiled. Once again, Ashley was amazed at the striking violet blue eyes all three of them possessed. Angel eyes—that was how Ashley thought of them.

Katie, always trying to seem cynical and skeptical, often scoffed that they were simply three oddball siblings who lived in the woods. Their eyes, she said, were simply the result of some strange gene they had in common.

It was certainly not any more incredible than believing they were angels.

But Ashley did believe they were angels. And she was shy and nervous around them.

A person didn't just *chat* with angels!

Ashley felt she should always say something deep and meaningful to them, yet her mind would go disturbingly blank, so she always wound up saying very little.

"Look who's here!" Ned said fondly to his companions.

Norma, the black-haired woman, waved, somehow managing to transform her face into a warm smile while barely moving her strong features. As Norma smoothed the hair wisping about her face, Ashley noticed the intricate, high-tech black digital watch she always wore. It seemed so out of place with her old-fashioned outfit.

"Hello, girls. How are you?" Edwina asked warmly, her beautiful, luminous face breaking easily into a wide smile.

Somehow, when Edwina asked, Ashley always felt she really wanted to know. So she thought about it. Although she did feel shy, she forced herself to answer. It would have been rude not to.

She decided everything was really all right with her. "Fine," she replied in a choked, small voice.

Edwina smiled and gazed at Ashley as if she were seeing something more than the physical appearance of a petite, redheaded thirteen-year-old girl. "Yes," she said. "I see that you are. And you, Katie. How are things with you?"

"Fine," Katie said, peering hard at the trio, her amber brown eyes bright with questions. Katie hated to admit they were truly angels, but she was completely fascinated by them. She'd even begun to write a story about them, imagining what their life was like here in the woods.

Ashley craned her neck to see what they were looking at so avidly within their circle. Ned stepped aside, allowing her to view three lovely wooden sailboats. They had red, white, and blue hulls with white cloth sails. "They're caught in an eddy," Ned explained matter-of-factly.

The girls and Champ came closer to the water. The three boats sailed steadily in a circle, caught in the spinning water where it collected between several low rocks that jutted just above the surface. "Why don't you just pick up the boats and set them back into the creek?" Christina wanted to know.

"Can't do that," Norma said, intently watching the boats.

"Why not?" Christina asked.

"It's not natural," Ned answered. "They have to find their own way."

"But what if they spin like that forever?" Ashley asked, finding her voice in her curiosity.

"They won't," Norma said with great confidence.

"It's just like with people," Edwina explained. "They sometimes get stuck moving in circles. It can last a long time and——"

"These boats have been circling since last week," Ned interjected.

"Last week!" Ashley gasped.

"Was it last week or last year?" Edwina asked Ned. "I get so confused about this time thing."

"Last week," Norma assured her.

"Well, anyway, these little boats have been going in circles for a while, just like people do when they get caught up in bad situations or confused about things in their minds," Edwina went on. "So we're studying how that works. It's amazing. There's just so much to learn."

As she spoke, one of the boats broke free of the circle. Champ barked excitedly as it floated downstream, rushing away from them.

"Yes!" Ned cheered, punching the air.

"Why did that one break free?" Christina asked, eager to understand.

"Something happened," Norma replied.

"What kind of something?" Christina asked. "Do you know?"

Ned shrugged. "Well, in this exact instance, a dragonfly skimmed the water, creating a ripple that traveled downstream and was broken by a twig in the water, the bottom half of which hit the boat's bow and bounced it out of the circle. Now the lucky little soul is back in the mainstream."

The word *soul* struck Ashley. Had he used it on purpose or simply as an expression?

"Eventually, something always happens," Norma said.

Edwina sighed. "It can take so awfully long sometimes."

At that moment, Norma's watch emitted a loud beep. She checked the watch as she shut off the alarm. Ashley noticed for the first time that it had many more dials than the usual watch face. "We've got to go," Norma told the others.

"Is it 1929 again already?" Edwina asked, seeming surprised.

"Maybe I should change and go to Wall Street," Ned suggested.

"Good idea," said Norma. "You get the jumpers, we'll get the others."

When Ashley looked back from Norma to Ned, he had somehow changed into an old-fashioned brown business suit. Norma sloshed out of the water beside him. "Bye, girls," Ned said as he and Norma walked into the woods and disappeared behind some pines.

Edwina lingered, gazing at the two remaining boats as they circled one another.

"Come on!" Norma's disembodied voice filled the air.

The girls turned in every direction trying to figure out where the voice was coming from. Even Champ cocked an ear and his browline dipped quizzically.

Edwina looked up sharply. "I'd better go," she said apologetically to the girls. "Never let money be your ruler," she sighed, shaking her head wearily as she headed out of the creek. "Money. It's just . . . just . . . nothing."

"You need money to live," Ashley said. Somehow she found Edwina easier to talk to than the other two.

"You need *life* to live," Edwina countered.

"It's about to crash!" Now Ned's voice filled the air.

Katie grabbed Ashley's shoulder in alarm. "What's crashing?" she gasped, sheltering her head with her other hand.

Edwina looked up. "I'm coming," she called to the air. "Ashley, you'll find the angelbloom by the bridge as always. Just remember one thing, though."

"Edwina!" Norma's urgent voice floated toward them on a breeze.

"I'll take the shortcut," Edwina said, hurrying behind the tall boulder on the edge of the creek.

"Remember what?" Ashley called after her. "What?"

Edwina's voice came from behind the boulder. "Don't rush things!"

Ashley turned to Christina, who had taken off her sneakers and rolled up her jeans so she could wade into the creek.

"What does that mean?" Ashley asked her. She kicked off her shoes and splashed through the water to the other side of the boulder. "What does that . . ." Her voice trailed off.

Edwina was gone.

". . . mean?" she finished softly.

"They do come and go abruptly," Katie noted dryly as she lowered her protective hand from over her head.

"I guess they had to go fast," Christina said, still staring at the circling boats. "It was crashing, after all."

"What?" Katie cried in frustration. "What was crashing?"

Christina shrugged, not taking her eyes off the little ships. "Something. Sounded like something big, too."

"The *Titanic!*" Ashley said, clapping. "That big ocean liner that crashed into an iceberg. I bet they were going back to save those people."

"Can angels go back in time?" Katie questioned.

"I don't know," Ashley admitted.

"Why not?" said Christina. "You know what I always think? Time is like a movie theater with the same—"

"Movie playing on a lot of screens, each screen showing a different part," Katie moaned. "I know! I know!"

"Well, okay, so why couldn't they move through time? They're spirits, after all," Christina said.

"Then maybe it was the *Titanic* they were going to," Ashley said.

"When did the *Titanic* sink? I don't think it was 1929, was it?" Katie noted seriously.

"Maybe they weren't supposed to get saved," Christina said quietly as she watched the boats. As she spoke, the second one slipped out of the eddy and rushed off sideways downstream.

The little boat careened into a rock sitting in the middle of the creek and fell on its side. Its wet sail floundered a moment before pulling the boat completely over, its small wooden centerboard pointing at the sky.

The girls looked at one another as the boat bobbed there helplessly. "Just turn it over," Katie told Christina. "I bet it will still float even though the sails are wet."

Christina shook her head. "I'd better not. You know what Ned said. It might upset their experiment."

"Let's find the angelbloom and go back. I have to get to work," Katie said in a grumbly voice. Casting a scowl at the boat—Ashley could see Katie was dying to free it—Katie began heading up the embankment.

"Come on," Ashley said, quickly jamming her feet back in her shoes as she began following Katie.

Christina left the creek, put on her sneakers, and caught up with them by the bridge's entrance.

With two fingers, Ashley whistled for Champ. He still lingered by the water's edge, looking around as if he was trying to figure out where the voices had come from. At the sound of her whistle blast, he scurried up the embankment to join them.

On the right side of the bridge, they found tall, sturdy

stalks with fat leaves at the bottom and round, green, tightly closed buds all along the tops of the stems. "This is it," Ashley said.

"How can you tell?" Christina asked. "The buds are shut tight."

"This is where they were growing the last time," Ashley said. "Yes, look. See, down by the water in that sunny spot? Some have already opened. Those are angelbloom, for sure." She hurried through the field of tall stalks down to the open flowers by the water.

The swaying flowers resembled the purple heather that grew wild around Pine Ridge, blooming usually in late August. Only these flowers weren't all purple. The undersides of the petals were a vivid pink. The flowers' two-tone petals made them seem to flicker and magically shift color as they danced in the light breeze that came off the creek.

Ashley snapped one stem. She had to bend and twist it to pull the sturdy stem apart. A milky liquid dribbled onto her hands.

The flower gave off a heady roselike aroma. Mingled with the odor of moist earth beneath her feet and the deep, rich smell of the pines, it flooded Ashley's senses. She shut her eyes and let the scents wash through her.

"It's great here, isn't it?" Christina said as Ashley opened her eyes.

Ashley nodded. It *was* great there. So peaceful and good. It was a place out of time where everything seemed possible.

"Help me pick these," Ashley asked. "I don't know how long the flowers last and I want enough for Dr.

Jeffers to work with."

The girls set to work picking the angelbloom flowers. "I wonder what crashed," Katie murmured as she worked. "What could possibly have crashed?"

4

"The stock market," Molly Morgan said as she closed the gray door to her school locker. She tossed back her long, silky white-blonde hair. "The stock market crashed in October of 1929. I'll bet you anything that's what they were talking about." Ashley, Katie, and Christina had just finished telling her about their encounter by the bridge.

"The stock market, of course," Ashley said, her back pressed against a locker. "That's right."

"Wow! I didn't know you were so good in history," Katie said as she shifted the brim of her baseball cap from the front to the back.

"Well, I just happen to know about that because it's part of my family history in a way," Molly explained. "My great-grandfather jumped out the window of his office the day the stock market crashed. He'd lost all his money and he didn't know what else to do."

"How horrible!" Christina gasped, clasping her hand to her chest in horror.

The girls began walking toward homeroom together.

"It would have been horrible except this weird thing happened," Molly said. "On his way down, an awesome wind came along and blew him right into an awning hanging over a window."

"What great luck!" Katie said as they wove their way through the flow of other middle school students hurrying toward homeroom.

"Yeah, and wait until you hear the rest," Molly went on. "While he's sitting in the awning, kind of dazed, I guess, a man climbs out one of the upper windows and comes down and sits with him in the awning. He talks to him for hours and tells him that if he goes home today, he'll find a reason to keep living."

"Did he?" Christina asked.

Molly nodded. "That very day when he went home, my great-grandmother told him that they were expecting a baby. The baby would be my grandmother, and she was their only child. My great-grandmother, Nanny, tells that story almost every time the family gets together." Molly paused and stooped over, imitating the stance of an old woman. She spoke in a creaky high-pitched voice. "'If it wasn't for that courageous young man who came out onto the awning, your grandmother wouldn't have had a father. I remember it like it was yesterday. Tuesday, October twenty-ninth, nineteen hundred and twenty-nine.'" Molly straightened, resuming her usual voice and posture. "And that's how I know exactly when the stock market crashed."

"What happened to your great-grandfather after that?" Katie asked.

"He did fine. For a while they were poor, and Nanny

even had to do wash for a hospital to make money. My great-grandfather helped her, and the next thing, they were running a chain of dry-cleaning places. They wound up richer than they had been before."

Katie laughed. "What a great story. And to think it's all because of that wind and the guy who climbed out the window."

"I wonder if the man wore a brown suit," Christina said quietly.

"I bet he did," Ashley agreed, knowing Christina was thinking of Ned.

"What?" Molly asked. They explained to her how Ned had changed into a brown business suit. Molly's thin face paled as she spoke and her hazel eyes went wide. "I wonder if it was Ned who saved him," she said. "What a thought. Maybe I can find out."

Molly reached into her large black straw shoulderbag and pulled out a small black cellular phone that her parents had given her for her thirteenth birthday. She quickly dialed a number. "Hi, Grandma, it's me, Molly. Yes, everything's fine. I'm at school."

They were just outside their homeroom. Some of the kids stared at Molly as they went inside.

"Order me a slice with double pepperoni," joked a boy with a blonde buzz cut named Darrin Tyson.

"Grandma, you know that story Nanny always tells about the day your dad jumped off the . . . yeah, that one," Molly spoke, ignoring Darrin. "Does she know what the man who came out on the awning looked like?" Molly tucked the phone under her chin. "She's asking her. Nanny lives with Grandma."

Tall, dark-haired Mr. Palmero, their homeroom teacher, came by. "Into the classroom, girls," he ordered pleasantly.

"One minute," Molly said, the phone still under her chin.

Mr. Palmero looked at her sternly. Ashley grabbed her free wrist and tugged her through the door. "And cut the phone call short, please," Mr. Palmero added. "Meaning right now."

Molly put the phone behind her back. "Sure," she said.

The girls took their assigned seats. Ashley sat a few seats in front of Katie in the last row by the window. Christina was up farther in the next aisle and Molly was all the way on the other side by the blackboard.

As Mr. Palmero took attendance, Ashley couldn't stop glancing sideways at Molly. She kept bending over as if she'd dropped something, whispering into the phone.

"Say good-bye, Ms. Morgan," Mr. Palmero demanded sharply.

"Good-bye, Grandma," Molly said quickly.

Moments later, a folded note was passed to Ashley by a girl beside her. Ashley unfolded it and read: *He did have on a brown suit. And he had strange eyes!!!!!!!!!!!*

Ashley passed the note back to Katie, who gasped as she read it.

For the rest of the morning, Ashley thought about the angels. Did they really move through time magically? It was odd to think how things that happened then affected things right now. Molly's family was rich now. But if her great-grandfather hadn't lived, maybe they would be poor. At least her mother's side of the family might have been poor. If Molly's mother had been poor, would she have met Molly's father? Possibly not. Would Molly be here if they didn't meet? Once you started thinking this way, you could go on and on.

Ashley kept remembering how the tiny ripple made by the dragonfly eventually caused the first boat to break free of the eddy and sail downstream.

By the time she got to science class, she was still lost in thought. But her teacher, Ms. Perez, a short woman with tight brown curls around her long face, was unusually excited today. The enthusiasm in her voice made Ashley put aside her thinking and pay attention.

"For the very first year ever, Pine Ridge Middle School will have a science fair. This is very exciting because we're competing with other districts this year. The winners from each school will go to a district science fair," she said.

"Thrills," Darrin muttered sarcastically from behind Ashley.

Ashley wasn't that thrilled, either. By the end of May, she was already thinking about summer. The idea of having to do a final big project for science wasn't good news. Christina, Katie, and Molly were lucky. They had different teachers. But maybe they'd have to do a project, too.

"The projects will count as twenty-five percent of your grade and will take the place of a final exam," Ms. Perez continued. "So make them good. Since we're covering biology, I'd like them to be in that category."

"Could I do an exploding volcano?" asked a heavy-set girl named Candy Martin.

"No, that's earth science," Ms. Perez told her. "I want biology projects, projects that have to do with living creatures—animals, people, plants."

"Could I cut up a frog?" Darrin called out.

"If you follow the proper procedure, yes," Ms. Perez replied tartly.

Pretty Rhonda Lynbrook, beside Darrin, made a disgusted face. "You're gross, Darrin."

Ashley went back to thinking about the angels. She was only half listening when Ms. Perez told them that by the end of class, she wanted each of them to submit an idea for a science project. She gave them time to flip through their textbook for ideas. Ashley opened her textbook but couldn't concentrate. Instead, she doodled in her notebook. She drew the angelbloom they'd picked the other day. She sketched an angel with wings, holding a bouquet of the flowers. Pleased with the sketch, she expanded it, drawing the ranch below the angel and a picture of Junior, the colt who'd recovered after eating the blossoms. She wasn't quite as happy with her rendering of Junior. Horses were hard to draw, she decided.

"Ashley . . ." An expectant voice floated to her as she erased Junior's tail to try it again. "Ashley..."

Ashley's head shot up and her hand spread over her sketch.

"Do you want to tell us what you've decided on?" Ms. Perez asked.

Ashley felt stuck. "Uh . . . um . . ."

"Well, I see you've been taking notes," Ms. Perez said. "What have you been writing?"

Ashley glanced down at her sketch. It gave her an idea. "I . . . um . . . was thinking about plants," she said honestly. "Plants that heal."

"The medicinal properties of plants and flowers!" Ms. Perez cried, clapping her hands with delight. "Wonderful. Did you know that heart medicine comes from the digitalis plant? And Chinese herbalists have been using gingko and ginseng for centuries. It's a fascinating subject. What a good idea!"

"Thanks," Ashley said quietly.

"What made you think of it? We haven't covered it in class," Ms. Perez asked.

"It just sort of came to me," Ashley said, not wanting to tell the whole story in front of the entire class.

"May I see your notes?" Ms. Perez asked, her dark eyes alight with excitement. She came alongside Ashley and gazed down at her notebook. Ashley had no choice but to move her hand.

Now I'm in trouble, Ashley thought. But Ms. Perez just frowned slightly, then nodded. "We all come by our ideas differently," she said. "I'm certainly looking forward to seeing your project."

Ms. Perez went on to talk to Darrin about the correct procedures for capturing a frog and killing it. Ashley didn't want to listen. She felt too sorry for the frog.

Instead, she thought about her project. It might be interesting, after all. In fact, she was suddenly very excited and eager to begin working on it.

5

"You're lucky to have a project you want to work on," Christina said later that afternoon as she and Ashley perused the shelves of the health food store in the Pine Ridge Mall. As it turned out, Ashley wasn't alone. All the eighth graders had to work on a project for the science fair.

"Mr. Donovan won't let me do anything on astrology since he says it's not a science," Christina complained while casually reading the label on a jar of something called EnergyVit. "He won't let me do crystals because he says the healing power of crystal energy is just an idea that has never been proven. He said I could do something on ESP, but I'd have to do all sorts of studies to see how people who got answers right by guessing compared with people who claimed to have clairvoyant powers."

"That sounds fair," Ashley said as she pulled a book titled *The Essential Herb Handbook* from the shelf and cracked its cover.

"Boring!" Christina grumbled, rolling her sky-blue eyes. "Who wants to do all those studies to prove something I already know is true?"

Ashley didn't have to ask how Christina knew. She was aware of Christina's amazingly accurate intuitions about things. She couldn't predict hurricanes, earthquakes, deaths, or lottery numbers, but she did seem to have an uncanny sixth sense for small things. She knew when someone might show up unexpectedly, or she'd call up Ashley at times when Ashley felt lonely or sad, somehow knowing she was needed.

Christina took a smooth white stone from the shelf. "I wonder if he'd let me do something on crystal deodorants," she said, silently reading the label on the bottom, which claimed the crystal would stop underarm odor naturally.

"Maybe he would," Ashley agreed. "Would that be biology or earth science, though? Ms. Perez says we have to stay with biology."

"Mr. Donovan says we can do anything, just not anything *I* want to do."

"He didn't say that," Ashley laughed. She scanned the contents page of her book. Alfalfa, black cohosh, cayenne, eyebright, red clover, saw palmetto berries, yarrow, yellow dock. There were so many herbs to learn about! And those were just the ones listed under the chapter titled "Vitamin A."

Curious, Ashley flipped to the index in the back of the book and looked under *A* for angelbloom. It wasn't there. She pulled out another book and again turned to the index. No angelbloom there, either.

"Can I help you find something?" A pleasant voice made Ashley look up from her book. A good-looking young man stood in front of her.

"I'm looking for information on angelbloom," she told him.

He shook his head. "Angelbloom? Don't know it. Are you sure you have the name right?"

"Positive," Ashley said. "It was in a book about herbal medicines, but there wasn't much information on it. I thought I could find something more."

The young man beckoned her to follow him to a computer at the front of the store. He typed in the word *angelbloom*. "Ah, here it is," he said. "Angelbloom." He pushed another button. "'It grows in Tibet,'" he read from the computer. "'Known to have antibiotic properties.'"

"Anything else?"

"That's it," he said. "There's not even a book listed here for where you can find more information."

"Dr. Jeffers, our vet, has a book listing it. That's where I found it before."

"It's probably an old book, out of print, otherwise it would be here," he told her. "What is this angelbloom stuff, anyway?"

"It's a flower that cured our colt when nothing else could."

"You got it all the way from Tibet?" he asked.

"Actually, I found it—"

Christina bumped into Ashley, cutting her off in mid-sentence. "Oh, sorry," she murmured. Ashley could tell the bump had been intentional. "We were lucky to get the flower from Tibet," Christina told the young man. "But we don't know if we'll be able to get any more. The company that ships it, the uh . . . Tibetan Shipping Company, went out of business. I think their rope bridge across the mountains broke or something."

Ashley raised her eyebrows as Christina spoke. Had she gone nuts?

"We have to get going," Christina said, pulling Ashley away. "Bye."

"Thanks for your help," Ashley said as Christina pulled her from the store.

"If you find out anything more, call and let me know," the young sales clerk called after her. "I'd be interested. Ask for John."

"Okay, John," Ashley called back as Christina pulled her through the door.

Outside the store, she yanked her arm out of Christina's grasp. "What was that all about?"

"Ashley, you don't want to tell people the angelbloom is growing in Pine Ridge," she scolded. "They'll be all over the woods looking for it. The woods would be spoiled. Maybe the angels would even leave."

"It wouldn't have hurt to tell him," Ashley disagreed. "He was nice."

"He works in a health food store," Christina argued. "He's the worst possible person to tell. People would come in and ask about cures and he'd tell them to go yank up some angelbloom over in the woods at Pine Manor Ranch."

"He would not," Ashley huffed. "You're being ridiculous."

"No, I'm not," Christina insisted.

Alice, Christina's mother, joined the girls. "Ready to

go?" she asked. The girls said they were and walked with Alice out to the parking lot where her brown pickup truck was parked.

"Why so quiet?" Alice asked as they drove down the winding road approaching the ranch.

Ashley had been thinking about the angelbloom. How could she keep quiet about it if she was going to use it in her science project? Besides, Dr. Jeffers wanted to write a paper about it. Soon everyone would know about it. What was the sense in trying to keep it a secret anyway? "I was thinking about my science project," Ashley said.

"I was just thinking about the woods," Christina replied, her voice overlapping Ashley's. "I was thinking how old they seem. I wonder how long the woods have been there."

"A very long time, I would imagine," Alice answered as she pulled into the ranch. "I suppose an expert could tell exactly, by looking at the trees."

"Deep in the woods, some of the trees are humongous," Christina said. "They've probably been there hundreds of years." She looked meaningfully at Ashley. "Centuries! It would be a shame if anything happened to ruin the woods."

Ashley looked out the window.

Alice drove past her own home and dropped Ashley off in front of her house. "See you tomorrow," Christina said as Ashley climbed down out of the truck.

"Tomorrow," Ashley replied. As she walked up onto the porch, Champ looked up from his nap. "Hi, fella," she said, ruffling the soft fur between his ears. "How's it going?"

He licked her hand to say how glad he was to see her. Ashley opened the door but froze before stepping inside. Her brother Jason was shouting angrily. "It's not fair!"

"Watch your tone of voice," Mr. Kingsley said sternly.

"Sorry," Jason said sullenly, "but it's not fair."

Gingerly, Ashley shut the door behind her and stepped inside. In the kitchen, just off the living room, her parents were sitting at the kitchen table across from her red-headed twin brothers, Jeremy and Jason.

What wasn't fair? she wondered, though the tension on their faces warned her not to barge right in and ask. Instead, she stood in the living room silently and listened.

"You could have told us," said Jeremy, who was the more mild-mannered of the twins.

"We didn't know," Mrs. Kingsley said, brushing a hand anxiously through her short, strawberry-blonde hair. "The ranch's finances are much better since we opened the inn, but we still owe money to a lot of people. We thought we could send you guys to college in the fall, but we just can't. I went over the finances with Dad last night and it's simply not possible right now."

"When will it be possible?" Jason grumbled.

"Maybe the fall after this one. Maybe the winter after that. We can't say for certain. It all depends how the ranch does during that time. And that will depend partly on you guys. We'll need you to work with us."

Jason jumped up, knocking the kitchen chair over behind him. "Oh, great! Not only am I stuck at home while all my friends go to college, but I have to work here."

"Pick up that chair!" Mr. Kingsley commanded, his voice growing angry. "We are doing our best, Jason. I

never went to college at all. It wasn't even a considera-
tion because there was no money for it and my family
needed the money I could make working. But you're
going to go. We'll get you there, it's just a matter of when."

"Yeah, like never!" Jason growled. "I'm going to be
stuck on this ranch forever, just like you."

"Jason!" Mr. Kingsley warned. "I said we will get you
there. In the meantime, you will have to work. We'll have
to take out loans, but we'll do it. We just need you to
wait, to be patient. Don't think we like this any more
than you do, because we hate it, too."

This obviously didn't make Jason feel any better. He
righted the chair, then stormed out of the kitchen and
past Ashley without even seeing her. Ashley felt the
anger coming off him like actual heat waves as he went
by.

"He's just bummed out," Ashley heard Jeremy say as
he, too, got up from his chair. "He'll get over it."

"I hope so," Mrs. Kingsley said, sounding depressed.

"He'd better get over it," Mr. Kingsley grumbled.

Jeremy walked past Ashley, his shoulders slumped.
"Hi, Ashley," he mumbled.

"Hi," she said, feeling terrible for him. Jeremy and
Jason had both been so psyched about going off to
college. Even though Jason was acting like a spoiled brat,
she knew it was just because he was so disappointed.

Her parents came out of the kitchen next. Her father's
deeply lined face was expressionless. Her mother looked
weary. Ashley felt sorry for them, too. She knew how
worried they'd been about money. Obviously, though
things were better, their worries weren't completely over.

Mr. Kingsley nodded a greeting to Ashley and headed into the den off the other side of the living room, which served as an office for the ranch.

"Hi, sweetie," Mrs. Kingsley said when she saw Ashley standing there. "How was the mall?"

"Okay," Ashley answered her mother.

Mrs. Kingsley forced a smile. "Good." Then she joined Mr. Kingsley in the den, shutting the lace-curtained French doors behind her.

Ashley was heading to her room down the hall when she stopped, hit by a sudden, awful realization. She was only four years younger than her brothers. By the time she was ready for college, they'd still be in school, especially if they were delayed by a year or two.

She couldn't imagine her parents having the money to send *three* kids to college at the same time. It meant she'd have to wait, too. And after her two brothers went to college, maybe she'd have to wait a long time before her parents were able to save enough money for her.

It took more than four years to become a veterinarian. She wasn't sure how much longer, but she was sure it was more than four years of college.

There might not be enough money left to send her to college at all! Ashley suddenly felt as if all her dreams were going up in smoke. How could she ever hope to become a veterinarian when she couldn't even go to college?

6

As Jason drove away down the long country road, his old car spewing a cloud of smoke behind it, Ashley stood and gazed up at Dr. Jeffers's square, stately, three-story red-brick home. It seemed out of place here on this road, bordered only by trees and wildflower fields. Its gleaming white shutters shone in the sunlight. White window boxes at the first-floor windows spilled over with sunny daffodils.

Walking up the stone stoop to the heavy red door, Ashley lifted the shiny brass knocker and banged. After two or three minutes, no one had answered. She was sure Dr. Jeffers had told her to come today, but she began to worry that she'd somehow gotten it wrong.

Nervously, she crumpled the top of the brown bag in her hands. It was filled with angelbloom. If Dr. Jeffers wasn't here, what could she do? It was too far to walk home. But what other choice did she have?

She walked around the side of the house on a slate walkway. A waist-high stone wall surrounded a slate patio on which sat a chair and table. Plants of all kinds flourished along the wall. Some were in large wooden containers, others crept up trellises beside the wall. An abundant vine full of long, tubular pink flowers grew along iron rods over the patio making a gorgeous natural outdoor roof. A willow basket of pink heart-shaped flowers sat on the patio table.

Ashley looked around. "Hello, anyone home?" The complete silence made the lovely place seem a little spooky. "Anyone home?" she repeated softly.

Behind her a twig snapped.

Startled, Ashley turned and cried out in fright.

A woman was *right* behind her, barely a foot away. Ashley panted hard. "You scared me!" How had the woman come up so silently?

"Sorry," the woman said. She was short and of indeterminate age. Her mid-length yellow hair was carelessly clipped to one side in a barrette. Thick-lensed rimless glasses gave her blonde-lashed blue eyes a starey expression. She wore a baggy light blue dress and scuffed black flats. "Is there something I can do for you?" she asked mildly.

"I'm . . . uh . . . I'm looking for Dr. Jeffers."

The woman took the willow basket from the table. "I'm Clematis. Come with me," she said mysteriously. Ashley followed her through a worn wooden door and into a cool, dark hallway.

They passed a large room whose open door revealed an old-fashioned desk with a wall of books behind it. Ashley followed the woman into a sunny room farther down the hall.

Dr. Jeffers stood in this room, facing a wall lined with metal cages. As they entered, she turned to greet them. She held a wiry young ferret in her hands. "Ashley," she said with a welcoming smile. "Hello."

"Hi," Ashley said, surprised to hear a nervous timber to her voice. She'd never been nervous around Dr. Jeffers before. Maybe it was because this was her first day on the job and she wanted so badly to do well, to justify Dr. Jeffers's faith in her.

"I see you've met Clematis," Dr. Jeffers said.

Clematis nodded politely at Ashley. "I'll put the bleeding hearts in water," she said to Dr. Jeffers.

Ashley looked wide-eyed at Dr. Jeffers. Pictures of bloody animal hearts sprang into her mind.

The veterinarian laughed, understanding Ashley's reaction. "Those flowers," she explained, gesturing with her chin toward the basket Clematis held. "They're called bleeding hearts."

"Oh," Ashley sighed with relief. "I didn't know. They're pretty."

Dr. Jeffers gently set the ferret back into its cage. "This is our examining room and holding area," she explained. "Overnight patients stay here." There were about sixteen cages in all, most of them empty. Besides the ferret, there was a tiger-striped cat, a poodle, and a very large fluffy white rabbit.

In a tall wire mesh cage off to the side of a window, a four-foot iguana perched on the branch of a small tree.

"What's up?" said an odd, high-pitched voice behind Ashley.

Ashley whirled around to see a large white cockatoo

sitting on top of a cage as tall as Ashley.

"That's Too-too," Dr. Jeffers said. "He's mine. So is Lizzy, the iguana. Their owners couldn't keep them anymore so I took them."

"I thought you only took care of farm animals," Ashley said.

"Most veterinarians do specialize, either doing large animals or smaller ones, but my father was a vet and he always did both, so I just followed in his footsteps. You see, back then he was the *only* vet in this entire area so he didn't have the luxury of specializing. I enjoy dealing with all kinds of animals, anyway. I'd hate to be limited. People even bring me wild animals that have been injured. It keeps things interesting for me."

"I love your house," Ashley said sincerely.

"Thank you. I grew up here. When Dad died, I took over his practice. Mom and Dad had this house built themselves, long before there were many other houses or stores in Pine Ridge."

Ashley suddenly remembered the bag she held in her hands. "I picked some angelbloom for you," she said, offering the bag.

Dr. Jeffers took it and opened it. She spilled the somewhat wilted flowers onto a white porcelain table by the door. "Thank you. Let's get these in water," she said. "I don't want to lose them."

"I had them in water," Ashley said, embarrassed by the droopy condition of the flowers. "But I guess they kind of conked out on the ride over."

"I think they'll revive easily enough," Dr. Jeffers said, picking up the angelbloom. "Come with me."

She led the way back through the hall to a plain, neat white kitchen with stainless steel cabinets. "This is the office kitchen," she explained as she reached high into a cabinet and pulled down a tall glass vase. "I live upstairs."

"I have more angelbloom at home," Ashley said as Dr. Jeffers arranged the large bunch of flowers—four more had blossomed since Ashley had first picked them—in the vase. "I put them in freezer bags so that they'd keep. Mom always does that with vegetables from our garden."

"Good idea," Dr. Jeffers commended her. "There should be a lot more flowers here, though. Look how many unopened buds there are. They'll keep blossoming for a while. I'd like to take some seeds and see if I can grow any here."

Ashley nodded. She wondered if that would be possible. Or did the flower have to be near the bridge to grow? Ashley suddenly wondered if the flowers grew beside a Buddhist monastery or some other kind of sacred place in Tibet, just as they grew near a special place in the Pine Manor woods, the Angels Crossing Bridge.

"Is Clematis your assistant?" Ashley asked.

Dr. Jeffers laughed lightly. "I guess so."

"Aren't you sure?" Ashley asked.

"Well, yes. Yes, she is my assistant. I laughed because the way she came to be here was a little strange."

"How?" Ashley was curious about the woman. She seemed so quiet and odd, not at all the kind of person Ashley would have imagined as Dr. Jeffers's assistant. She'd have pictured some energetic college student in a crisp, white medical jacket, not this sloppily dressed woman.

A thoughtful expression came over Dr. Jeffers's face.
"My husband died five years ago, and it was a very
hard time for me. Emotionally, I was very low, very
sad. I wasn't really able to keep up with the demands
of my practice. One day, I felt so terrible that I didn't even
get out of bed all day. But, when I came downstairs that evening, the animals had all been tended
to—and there was Clematis. She'd taken care of them all."

"Do you mean she just walked in and started taking
care of them?" Ashley asked.

"More or less. She'd come to bring me a bird she'd found
that had a broken wing. When she got here, she thought
the animals in the cages had been abandoned and so she
simply did the kind and logical thing by taking care of
them. Still, many other people would have just left."

"So you hired her?"

"Not right away. When I came downstairs, still in my
nightgown, we started talking. I told her about Frank,
my husband, and what a struggle I'd been having. The
next day, when I came down, the animals had already
been taken care of. She came every day after that to help
me."

"That was nice," Ashley admitted, despite her wary
feelings about Clematis.

"It *was* nice and she never asked for pay. But after a
while, I felt I should pay her. It wasn't fair not to."

Carrying the angelbloom in a vase, Dr. Jeffers led the
way back to the room with the animals and cages.
Ashley followed, telling her how she'd tried to find more
information on the flower in the health food store, but
there hadn't been any. "Hmmm," Dr. Jeffers said

thoughtfully, setting the vase down on a side table near Lizzy. "It's in the book I have."

"The guy in the store said your book must be out of print."

Dr. Jeffers left the room and returned in few minutes with a heavy leather-bound book. "This book is quite possibly out of print," she said, opening it. "It was one of my father's books." She checked the copyright page. "This book was published in 1929."

"The same year as the stock market crash," Ashley murmured.

Dr. Jeffers looked surprised. "Yes," she said. "In the years afterward, during the Depression, times were tough. A lot of families were quite poor. Dad used to take care of animals for free sometimes. I was very young, but I still remember it. I'm surprised you remember the date. Are you studying it in school?"

"No. It just came up in a . . . a . . . a conversation," Ashley replied.

Looking impressed, Dr. Jeffers turned back to her book. She thumbed through it until she came to angelbloom. "No, there's not much here, it's true. A plant with antibiotic properties found in Tibet. Strange."

"It's like someone discovered it, and then everyone forgot about it," Ashley said.

"Probably because it was only found in Tibet," Dr. Jeffers agreed. "If you can't get an herb, what's the sense in studying it."

"That's true," Ashley said. "Only now we *can* get it."

Dr. Jeffers gently closed the book. "I think I *will* study it," she said. "I'd like to run some tests, and if I get the same amazing results as you got with Junior, I'll write a paper on it. People should know about this."

"This is exciting," Ashley said. The tests and their results would also be great information to use in her science project. It would make it really interesting.

"I agree. It's quite exciting," Dr. Jeffers said. "This could be a major contribution to veterinary medicine, maybe even to human medicine."

"Major discovery, eh? Do tell!" A young man stood in the doorway. He looked to be in his thirties and was dressed casually in a rumpled suit jacket and jeans. His blue sports shirt was open at the collar. His dark hair was mussed and it looked as if he hadn't shaved in a day or so.

"Mr. Peters, hello," Dr. Jeffers greeted him. "Is it noon already?"

"No, I'm early," he said, grinning as he walked into the room. "I like to come early. Catching people unawares sometimes produces an unexpected story. Like this one. What's the major discovery?"

"Mr. Peters is doing a story on me for the *County Gazette*," Dr. Jeffers explained to Ashley.

"That's right. Dr. Jeffers here is one of a kind. There's no one else like her in the county. She does things the old-time way," Mr. Peters drawled.

"And the modern way, too," Dr. Jeffers said pointedly. "I simply don't believe in over-medicating an animal if a hot compress or an herbal tea or the like will be just as effective, or more effective."

"Right," Mr. Peters said curtly. "Now what's the major discovery?"

"You certainly have a nose for news," Dr. Jeffers kidded.

"That's my job," Mr. Peters said evenly.

"There is no major discovery," Dr. Jeffers said. "Not yet, anyway. I'm looking into the medicinal properties of that flower over there. That's all. We don't know much about it yet, but a sick animal took it once, by accident, and recovered."

Mr. Peters took a hand-sized tape recorder from his jacket pocket and clicked it on. "Fluke accident reveals miracle medical wonder," he said into it.

Dr. Jeffers held up her hand. "No. Please, Mr. Peters. I really must ask you not to write anything about this yet. We really don't know anything."

"Okay. All right," he said, returning the tape recorder to his pocket. "Promise you'll keep me filled in. Breaking a story on a medical miracle is big news. It's the kind of story that could win a guy the Pulitzer Prize, you know."

Dr. Jeffers laughed indulgently. "Don't count your chickens before they hatch," she warned lightly.

"That's just what I'd expect a veterinarian to say," Mr. Peters teased. "But if something exciting is happening here, I want to know about it."

"I assure you, there's nothing exciting. Yet," Dr. Jeffers said.

Ashley wasn't so sure, though. She glanced at the flowers on their sturdy stems and felt the urge to rip them apart and find out what secrets lay within them. She couldn't wait to see what Dr. Jeffers's tests revealed. They were on the brink of uncovering something big. Earthshaking. Ashley felt it in her bones.

7

"How awesome!" Molly squealed. She unfolded the *County Gazette* on the cafeteria table. Katie and Christina huddled around her, gazing down at the story Ashley had brought in to show them. "Look, it even mentions you and everything."

"I know," Ashley said excitedly. "I didn't think Mr. Peters would put me in the story, but I was sitting there through the whole interview, so I ended up in it."

Dr. Jeffers was pictured sitting behind the desk in her library. The story told all about her life and her veterinary practice. "Turn the page," Ashley said.

Molly turned the page, revealing a picture of Ashley and Dr. Jeffers standing in front of the animal cages.

"Too cool!" Katie shouted, clapping her hands.

"It's a good picture of you," Christina commented.

"I should have worn a different shirt. That one looks wrinkled," Ashley commented critically.

"Oh, hardly," Katie scoffed. "That would be the day when you looked wrinkled."

"'Dr. Jeffers and her assistant, Ashley Kingsley, cure animal ills with herbal remedies. They're currently studying a new discovery that may prove to be a major breakthrough,'" Molly read the caption under the picture.

"He shouldn't have written that," Ashley said. "Dr. Jeffers asked him not to say anything about the angelbloom until we know more about it."

A buzzer rang, marking the end of the lunch period. Ashley folded the newspaper and stuck it under her arm as she followed her friends out the cafeteria door. They walked together until Ashley turned down a hallway to the right and went the rest of the way to her science class alone.

She was nearly there when Ms. Perez came up alongside her. "I saw your picture in the *County Gazette*, Ashley," she said. "It's wonderful that you're working with Dr. Jeffers. She's an amazing woman. Last spring she kept my brother from losing all his cows when they got sick. Now they're fine."

"Yeah, she's great," Ashley agreed. "I was really glad when she asked me to work for her."

"I'll bet," Ms. Perez said. "And now I understand why you chose the medicinal properties of plants as your project. I saw in the paper that you're working with Dr. Jeffers on something really big."

"Well . . . maybe," Ashley said, not sure that she should talk about it. But what would it hurt to tell Ms. Perez? "It's a flower I found in the woods by my house that might be a new herbal cure. But Dr. Jeffers wants to test it first."

"How exciting! I can't wait to see your project. I'll bet

it'll be a strong contender for the district finals. If you report on original research . . . well, that's almost a sure-fire win. The judges adore original research."

"Really?" Ashley asked as they stopped outside the classroom door.

"Absolutely. And you know, Ashley, the district prize is a college scholarship. I'm not sure of the exact amount, but it's a big one."

"A scholarship!" Ashley gasped. That was just what she needed if she was going to make it to college. It could solve all her problems. "That's great!" she said. "Really great."

Ms. Perez smiled. "Well, do a good job, and I think you'll have a real shot at it."

"Really!" Ashley breathed. She'd have to make sure Dr. Jeffers didn't waste time. She had to get her moving so she'd have original research to report on in time for the science fair.

* * *

Even though Ashley wasn't due to go back to Dr. Jeffers's until the next Saturday, she persuaded Jason to drive her over that afternoon. "I just thought I'd see if you need any help," she said breezily, popping her head into Dr. Jeffers's office.

"Wonderful," Dr. Jeffers said, looking up from the book she was reading. "You can help Clematis clean the cages."

Ashley wrinkled her nose. *Let Clematis clean the cages*, she thought. "Uh . . . Dr. Jeffers? Have you started the tests on the angelbloom yet?"

"Yes," Dr. Jeffers replied, "but it will take a few days to get the results."

"Oh," Ashley said disappointed. With a sigh, she walked toward the examining room with its cages.

"Ahh!" Ashley cried as the ferret scrambled over her feet the moment she stepped into the room.

Clematis turned away from an empty cage and stared at Ashley. "I'll put him back in as soon as his cage is done," she said in her flat, expressionless voice.

"That's okay," Ashley said. "He startled me, that's all."

"What's up!" Too-too squawked from on top of his cage.

Ashley smiled at him. "Want help with the cages?" Ashley offered, and was relieved when Clematis said they were all done. Back at the ranch Ashley often helped shovel out the stalls in the stable, which was actually far worse, but it was a job she always hated.

"Hand me the ferret, please," Clematis requested.

"Sure," Ashley said. The fuzzy weasel was in the corner, batting a piece of crumpled paper that had fallen from the overflowing wastebasket. "Come on, little guy," Ashley cooed as she walked toward him. The ferret scrambled away and ran behind a cabinet. "Now what do I do?" Ashley asked helplessly.

Clematis knelt by the cabinet. She held out her hand and made a soft clicking noise with her tongue. The skinny creature slithered out along the wall, ran to her, and leaped into her hands. Clematis scratched behind his ears as she lifted him.

"Wow!" Ashley said, impressed.

Clematis gave her a small, knowing smile. Instantly, Ashley felt annoyed by her superior attitude. Clematis had been working here a while. Of course the animals knew her better than they knew Ashley. In a week or so, she would be just as confident with these animals as she was with the horses at the ranch, Ashley told herself.

Clematis returned the ferret to its cage. As she walked past Too-too's cage, the cockatoo fluttered over and perched on her shoulder. Clematis reached up and petted him. "Pretty Clem!" the bird shouted. "Pretty Clem!"

Who taught him to say that? Ashley wondered as an irrational jealousy swept through her. Clematis was certainly not pretty. *She probably taught him that herself*, Ashley thought.

"Hello! Helll-ooooo!" a female voice called in a singsong from out in the hall. A tall, attractive woman in a white linen suit, her blonde hair pulled into a French braid, came into the room, cradling a lanky brown-and-beige Siamese cat in her arms. "Is Dr. Jeffers in?" she inquired of Clematis

Clematis put Too-too back on top of his cage in her usual, unhurried manner. Before she got around to answering, Dr. Jeffers walked in. "What can I do for you?" she asked the woman pleasantly.

"Something is the matter with Muffy," the woman explained, frowning. "She's a seal point. They're very expensive, very temperamental animals, you know. I took her to my vet in the city, but he simply had no idea what to do for her. I'm visiting my parents here in Pine Ridge and they recommended I come see you. They say you're the best."

Dr. Jeffers smiled at the compliment. "Thanks," she said, taking the languid cat from the woman. "What are Muffy's symptoms?"

"She won't eat. She has no energy. I'm very worried about her."

Dr. Jeffers put the cat on the examining table. With a penlight she examined its eyes and ears, then gently pried its jaws open to examine its mouth. "I'm going to have to run some tests," she said. "Can you leave her here a day or two?"

"Yes, all right. I'll be here for another week," the woman agreed. "Oh, I do hope you can help her. Muffy and I are so close. I don't know what I'd do without her."

Ashley thought the woman was silly and pretentious, but she felt sorry for her just the same. She could see that she *was* really attached to Muffy. Something in the way she gazed so anxiously at the animal made it clear that what pained her cat pained her, too.

"Clematis will take your name and Muffy's history in my office," Dr. Jeffers said to the woman. "I'll do my best by Muffy. And in the meantime, Ashley will make her comfortable here."

With a last, worried glance at her cat, the woman trailed Clematis out of the room.

"Prepare that large cage at the bottom with a bed, a cat box, and some water," Dr. Jeffers instructed Ashley as she prepared a syringe. "I'll start by running some blood tests."

"What do you think is wrong with Muffy?" Ashley asked as she opened a large bag of kitty litter standing next to a cabinet.

"Could be a virus or an infection. Could be worms. I'll have to take a blood and stool sample before I can be sure."

Ashley gazed at the listless cat who lay on the table, staring dully with blank, blue eyes, her head resting on her paws. "Why don't you try angelbloom on her?" Ashley suggested. "Remember how well it worked on Junior? No one knew what was the matter with him, either."

Dr. Jeffers shook her head. "I could never give it without knowing more about it. We must wait for the test results. Antibiotics can be very specific. What works for one illness may not be especially effective on another. It might have simply been luck in Junior's case."

"But what can it hurt?" Ashley pressed as she poured the litter into a plastic pan and put it in the cage.

"We don't know," Dr. Jeffers insisted, pulling on rubber gloves. With one hand on the cat's middle, she skillfully extracted a small amount of blood. Muffy flinched slightly, twisting, but Dr. Jeffers held her in a firm, confident grasp.

Ashley found a soft, worn pillow in a closet. She put it in the cage, then filled a water dish from the sink in the kitchen down the hall. She understood why Dr. Jeffers was being so cautious. It made sense to her. And yet, it was frustrating. How would they ever make any kind of breakthrough if Dr. Jeffers was too nervous to take a chance? They certainly wouldn't make one in time for her science project.

She finished preparing the cage while Dr. Jeffers cradled Muffy in her arms, gently picking through her fur. "I'm checking for any parasites," she explained. "But this cat doesn't even have fleas."

Clematis returned, holding a clipboard. "Here's the

information," she said. "Should I file it or leave it out for you?"

"Leave it out, please, Clematis. I want to go over it."

"Clematis," Ashley said, "don't you think Dr. Jeffers should try the angelbloom on Muffy?" Maybe if Clematis backed her up, Dr. Jeffers would change her mind.

"Absolutely not," Clematis disagreed. "That would be highly irresponsible."

That would be highly irresponsible, Ashley angrily mimicked Clematis in her head. What a drag she was! Her personality was every bit as frumpy as her appearance. Ashley didn't know *what* the animals liked about her.

They'll like me better soon, Ashley thought, once again seized with an irrational jealousy.

Clematis carried Muffy to the cage Ashley had prepared. The cat nuzzled her arm in the first show of affection Ashley had seen from the animal since its arrival.

Now that I'm here, Dr. Jeffers won't need Clematis anymore, Ashley thought. At once she was ashamed of herself for being so mean. She couldn't help it, though. Clematis bugged her. And Ashley was sure if she spent enough time around her she'd figure out why.

8

At six o'clock, Ashley phoned the ranch and asked if someone could come pick her up. "I'll send Jason," Mrs. Kingsley told her. As Ashley left Dr. Jeffers's office, she saw Clematis coming into the shadowy hallway from outside. She held something cupped in her hands.

Clematis's face was screwed into a concerned scowl. "A chipmunk," she explained when she saw Ashley looking. "I found it lying in the garden."

Ashley followed Clematis into the examining room.

"What have we got here?" Dr. Jeffers said, taking the limp little creature from Clematis. Carefully, she set it on the examining table. The chipmunk was panting, wide-eyed with terror, but too weak to run away. Its tiny, frail body quivered with fear.

"It's not bleeding or injured," Ashley noted.

"No," Dr. Jeffers agreed, stroking its back lightly with two knuckles. "I don't think there's much I can do for the little guy. Small animals like this are so fragile once they get sick."

"Why not try the angelbloom?" Ashley suggested.

"We don't really know how it works, or even *if* it works," Clematis reminded her.

Not that Ashley needed reminding. She *knew* how Dr. Jeffers felt, but this might be the exception, the chance to experiment. Clematis was so dull and slow. Ashley really wished she wasn't around all the time.

Ashley looked past Clematis to Dr. Jeffers. "The chipmunk will die anyway if we don't try."

"You may be right," Dr. Jeffers agreed slowly as she laid the chipmunk on a folded cloth and placed him in a cage. She closed the cage, went to the vase of flowers, and snapped off two blossoms. Clematis and Ashley accompanied her to the kitchen where she boiled a saucepan of water. As soon as it bubbled, she tossed in the flowers. "We'll let that cook for about five minutes so that the healing properties of the flower really infuse the water," she told them.

In five minutes, she poured the steaming water through a metal sieve into a tea kettle. The flowers had tinted the water a lovely light pink. "That has to cool a bit now," she said.

After another ten minutes, the three of them returned to the examining room. Dr. Jeffers drew a bit of the angelbloom tea into an eyedropper. Taking the chipmunk from the cage, she laid him on the examining table. "Okay, little guy, here you go," Dr. Jeffers said as she held him in her hand and squeezed three drops of the pinkish tea into his mouth.

Dr. Jeffers put the chipmunk back into his cage. "We'll just have to wait and see," she said.

"It took a while with Junior, but maybe it will work faster on the chipmunk," Ashley said, staring hard at the small animal, hoping to detect any sign of improvement. "If it works on the chipmunk, maybe you could try it on Muffy," she suggested.

"Slow down," Dr. Jeffers laughed. They both glanced at the Siamese cat lying listlessly in her cage. "I want to review her tests before I do anything. And I'm waiting for the test results on the angelbloom, too."

"But you'll at least think about using the angelbloom?" Ashley pressed eagerly.

Clematis frowned at Ashley, but said nothing.

"Let's see what happens with the chipmunk first," Dr. Jeffers said.

Despite her caution, Ashley felt encouraged. Now she'd taken the first step by giving the chipmunk the flower tea. The next step—Muffy—couldn't be far behind.

Looking away from Muffy, Ashley remembered that she'd called for a ride. "I'd better go out and wait for my brother."

"Thanks for coming by, Ashley," Dr. Jeffers said. "I'll see you Saturday."

"You're welcome." Ashley went out into the hall and out to the patio. She was surprised to see that although it was around seven o'clock, it was still light out. Spring was definitely here, and summer would be right behind. She couldn't wait to be done with school and to have time off. Of course she'd have to work at the ranch, at the inn and taking out trail rides, but that was fun, really. She could offer to spend more time with Dr. Jeffers, too.

Except for Clematis, Ashley loved it there. She

admired Dr. Jeffers and liked working with the animals. In just two visits, she'd become certain she wanted to be a veterinarian. Maybe she'd even work with Dr. Jeffers. She was getting older. She might want someone to take over her practice, just as she herself had taken over her father's veterinarian practice.

If only she could win that scholarship, Ashley thought longingly as she walked around to the front of the house. Then she'd know she could count on going to college. Working with the angelbloom would give her a great shot at it. She thought about Ms. Perez saying the judges went wild over original research. How many other kids would be in a position to present information on a new, thrilling discovery? Not many, Ashley bet.

She gazed down the long road, looking for Jason's old brown Chevette. Where was he? she wondered, pacing. She waited for fifteen minutes. The soft yellow-pink light melted into a dusky gray-blue. He was always so late.

A noise made Ashley turn toward the front of the house. Clematis was climbing onto an old bike. She began pedaling toward Ashley.

"Do you want a ride somewhere?" Clematis offered.

"No, thank you," Ashley declined politely. Riding on the back of Clematis's bike was just about the last thing she could picture herself doing. She wouldn't even want to be that close to her.

Clematis nodded and went on her way, biking down the road. Ashley watched her until she was just a speck in the distant, dying light. "Oh, Jason!" she fumed. Turning away from the road, she walked back to the patio. She'd use the phone inside to check if he'd even left yet.

Inside, it was quiet. Dr. Jeffers's office was empty. Ashley assumed she'd gone upstairs for the evening. As she stepped into the office to use the phone, a frantic, scurrying sound made her stop. It came from the examining room.

Curious, Ashley went to see what it was. She flipped on the light as she walked in. "What's up?" Too-too squawked from inside his cage.

"Oh, my gosh!" Ashley breathed in a hushed, awed tone.

The chipmunk was running around his cage, excitedly looking for a way out.

"You're better!" she cried, walking up to the cage. "It worked!"

As if in answer, the chipmunk sat up on his hind legs and complained to her, his sharp little bark surprisingly loud. He was absolutely full of energy and raring to go.

"Hey, you! Shut up!" Too-too bellowed, disturbed by the chipmunk chatter. "Hey, you! Shut up!"

Dr. Jeffers had to see this!

Ashley ran from the examining room to the stairs beside the office kitchen. She ran up and found herself in an elegant and old-fashioned living room. It was softly lit by a colorful Tiffany glass table lamp sitting on a curved cherrywood table by the lace-curtained front window. "Dr. Jeffers!" she called. "Dr. Jeffers."

No answer came. "Dr. Jeffers!" she called again.

Ashley heard a car engine coming from out in front of the house. Was it Jason? She hurried to the window to see. No. It was Dr. Jeffers driving away in her red Jeep.

Hmmmm. What to do?

She decided to leave Dr. Jeffers a note. In the rather plain, white kitchen she found a yellow pad held onto the refrigerator door by a magnetic cow. *Go look at the chipmunk. You won't believe it!* Ashley wrote, using the pencil tied to the cow's neck.

As she was leaving the kitchen she stopped, remembering she wanted to phone home. She was just about to lift the receiver of the white wall phone when it rang.

Ashley hesitated. Should she answer? Was there a phone machine?

She let it ring three times. No answering machine went on. Maybe she should pick it up and take a message. "Hello?"

"Is Dr. Jeffers there? This is Bill Peters."

"Mr. Peters! Hi! This is Ashley. Thanks for putting me in your article. Everyone was really impressed. My mother is framing it and hanging it in her office."

"No problem," he said. "Is Dr. J. around?"

"She just went out. Hey, listen! Something really exciting just happened!" Ashley was so glad to have someone to tell. This was so thrilling, she couldn't stand to keep it to herself. She told him all about how the angelbloom had cured the chipmunk. She rambled on, telling how she'd found it in the Pine Manor woods and how it had cured Junior. "It's only supposed to grow in Tibet, but there it was, right in our woods."

"How weird," he mused. "I wonder how it got there."

Ashley opened her mouth to tell him about the angels, but changed her mind. Either he wouldn't believe her—or he would. In either case, it would be better not to bring it up. If he believed it, he might write a story about it, and who knew where that would lead.

"Are you there, Ashley?" he asked.

"Yeah. Sorry. I was just thinking about something. Uh . . . should I give Dr. Jeffers a message?"

"Oh . . . yeah. My editor wants to talk to her about writing a column on animal care. Ask her to call me at the *Gazette,* would you?"

"Sure, I'll leave her a note."

"Thanks. And thanks for the scoop on the angelbloom. Bye."

"Bye." Ashley hung up and wrote *Call Mr. Peters* on the refrigerator pad. As she finished, two sharp blasts of a car horn blared from outside. Ashley recognized the sound of the horn. "It's about time, Jason," she muttered, running back downstairs to go out and meet him.

9

"You told a reporter about angelbloom!" Christina yelped. She jumped down from the rail fence she'd been sitting on and faced Ashley, still seated on the fence. "How could you do that?"

"I don't know. He called and I was so excited, I had to tell *someone*." Ashley watched a firefly blink off and on in the empty horse pasture. Soon several lit the warm night like tiny, winking flashlights. "What's the big deal?"

"He's a reporter. He's going to write about it," Christina said flatly.

"So?" Ashley was beginning to feel a little annoyed. It was easy for Christina to act so high and mighty. She hadn't been there. She hadn't seen what a miraculous effect the angelbloom had on that poor little chipmunk. In fact, it was beginning to bug her how Christina acted like she owned the angelbloom or something when after all, it was Ashley who had discovered it.

"Come on, Ashley, you know what we've talked about,"

Christina said. "Remember? About the woods and the . . . the angels?"

They'd agreed to keep everything about the angels a secret. If people found out how amazing the woods were, they'd come from all over and tramp around. They could even end up destroying the woods. Ashley and Christina knew that had happened with other places. That was why there were national parks and other protected areas. If the woods became overrun with people, the angels might even leave.

"Well, maybe we were wrong," Ashley said stubbornly. "Anyway, I didn't tell him anything about the angels," she added. "Just the flowers."

"It's practically the same thing!" Christina exploded. "It might even be worse. If angelbloom *is* a miracle medicine, people will want to grab it all up."

"Don't you think they have a right to know?" Ashley challenged her. "Who are we to keep something like this secret? I don't think *that's* very nice. What if it was your mother who was sick and someone knew something that would make her better, but they were keeping it a secret. How would you feel?"

This point stopped Christina. She frowned thoughtfully as she hopped back onto the fence, standing with her sneakers on the bottom rail and her hands grasping the top. "When you put it that way, I don't know. I mean, I suppose. Still . . . somehow . . . it doesn't seem right."

"Think about it, Christina," Ashley said, warming to the subject. "We might be famous. The Pine Manor Ranch will be the only place where people can come to get the angelbloom. They'll flock here, you know, like the way they go to Lourdes in France. We'll be on *60 Minutes* and *20/20* and all those shows. Barbara Walters will come to interview us. We'll be guests on *Oprah*."

"*Oprah?*" Christina laughed incredulously.

"Yeah. Why not? We'll be famous." Ashley swung her leg over the top rail so that she was facing Christina. She leaned forward excitedly. "We might even get rich."

"Why? Because all those people would be coming to the ranch?" Christina asked warily.

"Yes. And because we have the angelbloom. We could sell it."

A firefly flew past Christina and blinked. Its blinking matched the hard blinking of Christina's wide eyes. Her jaw dropped. She appeared thunderstruck.

"What?" Ashley wanted to know. "What's wrong?"

"You would *sell* the angelbloom?" Christina asked, horrified.

"Sure. Why not?"

"That flower is a gift from the angels. You can't sell it," Christina practically shouted.

Ashley shrugged. She didn't want to hear this. "My parents own that land. They own acres and acres of it, past the creek and over to the road. Whatever's on it is theirs."

"The angelbloom might belong to them legally, but do you think it's right to sell it?"

"Yes," Ashley said. "I do."

"I'm not so sure," Christina said slowly.

"Well, I am. What if the angels put that flower there exactly for this reason—to help my family? And you and your mother, too. If we get rich, it'll benefit you.

Wouldn't you like to live in a big house and have great stuff like Molly? Look how she gets whatever she wants. Think about the clothes she has. Wouldn't you want that?"

"It's not that important," Christina said.

No, Ashley considered, Christina was probably being honest. Material things didn't matter that much to her. Ashley also knew they weren't the *most* important things on earth, but she liked beautiful things. She loved fashionable clothing. And she'd seen how much unhappiness and stress not having enough money had brought her parents. At one point, they'd almost divorced over it. How wonderful it would be not to have to think about money anymore—to just forget about it because it was always there.

"Don't you want to go to college?" Ashley pressed.

"Sure I do," Christina said, "but you don't have to be rich to do that."

"You have to have enough money."

"I'll work. I'll get a loan."

"I suppose," Ashley conceded. "But then you'll be working all the time, and you'll have this giant loan to pay back."

"We're only thirteen. I'm not worrying about college now," Christina said. "Besides, we're talking about the angelbloom, not college."

"It's all tied up together." Ashley could see it all. The angelbloom project would win the science fair. She'd get the scholarship, but she might not even need it. Her family would make lots of money from the angelbloom. They'd have plenty to send Jason, Jeremy, and Ashley to great colleges. Ashley would become a veterinarian. After a while she'd take over Dr. Jeffers's column. Her fame would grow. She'd be invited on TV shows to talk about animals. She might even get her own animal show. She'd be famous. Rich and famous.

Wasn't that what everyone wanted? Why shouldn't she?

A breeze pushed her hair into her face. Ashley brushed it back and shivered. "I guess we should get home."

"I guess," Christina agreed.

"Don't be mad at me," Ashley said.

"I'm not. Not really," Christina said as the breeze played with her long, blond waves. "I suppose I'm more worried than mad. I don't want things to change here. I like them the way they are. And I don't want the angels to leave. It gives me a good feeling knowing they're so close."

Ashley hopped off the fence. "They won't leave."

"You can't be sure of that," Christina disagreed, sliding off the fence beside her.

*　　*　　*

The next afternoon, Dr. Jeffers called Ashley to say how excited she was over the chipmunk's recovery. "I will definitely write to the Association of Veterinary Medicine and let them know I'm testing the effects of the angelbloom. This is too important to delay."

"Great!" Ashley said as a new confidence coursed through her.

"I think I'll also write to the *Journal of Veterinary Medicine* and propose an article on the subject."

"Are you going to try the angelbloom on Muffy now?" Ashley asked.

"Well, no, not yet," Dr. Jeffers said. "Her test results still aren't in."

"But, Dr. Jeffers, you have to!" Ashley said. "You just said yourself it's too important to delay."

"That's true," Dr. Jeffers said. "On the other hand, I don't want to rush things and possibly make mistakes that could compromise the results we've already had."

"Oh," Ashley said, disappointed.

"Ashley, I know you're enthusiastic about the possibilities of angelbloom," Dr. Jeffers said, "and I am, too. But we have to make sure we do everything right."

"I know," Ashley said. She still thought Dr. Jeffers was being too cautious, especially after the flower worked on the chipmunk, but what could she do? "Are you going to let Mr. Peters know about it?"

"Yes, but not just yet. You didn't say anything more to him, did you, Ashley?"

Ashley swallowed hard. "Uh . . . I did tell him about the chipmunk when he called your house," she admitted. "I was so excited, I had to tell someone."

Dr. Jeffers sighed. "I wish you hadn't, but . . . all right. We'll just hope he doesn't write about it."

"Sorry."

"That's all right."

On Wednesday, Ashley longed to go over to Dr. Jeffers's and see what was happening, but no one was free to give her a ride after school. She contented herself with walking to the library and taking out books on herbs and herbal remedies. While she was browsing through the aisles, she saw a familiar face. It was the guy from the health food store in the mall, John.

"Hey, hi," he said with a friendly smile.

"Hi, John," she said.

"It's funny I ran into you," he said. "I was just talking about you with my friend Bill . . . Bill Peters. He says you and Dr. J. have been doing some interesting stuff with that angelbloom. Did you find out anything more about it?"

"Not really," Ashley said.

"Bill and I had an idea for a screenplay we want to write together. It's about your angelbloom."

"A screenplay. Wow!" Ashley said, impressed. "You know how to write movie scripts?"

"Yeah, I took a course on it in college. We had this idea to have a bunch of kids who see a spaceship, but the adults don't believe them because they can't see it, only kids can. And the spaceship scatters seeds all over the world. Then the adults get all freaked out about it, and they try to destroy the spaceship, but the kids have to stop them because they know— the aliens have told them—that when the seeds grow, the flowers will cure all kinds of sickness, you know, like angelbloom. Pretty exciting, huh? What do you think?"

"Exciting," Ashley agreed. If he only knew how the flowers really got here, he might think it was even more interesting, she considered.

"There's only one problem," he went on. "Bill and I have to get enough money together to quit our jobs so we have time to write the darn thing."

Ashley nodded sympathetically. "Not having money is a problem."

"It sure is," John agreed. "But I think we've got our problem solved," he added with a smile. He started walking away from her, down the aisle. "Thanks for the idea," he said.

"You're welcome," Ashley replied.

* * *

That Thursday, after school, Mrs. Kingsley drove into the small downtown area of Pine Ridge to pick up milk and a few other sundries. Ashley and Christina came along just for the fun of browsing.

They went into O'Herlihy's Market, a small country store that sold food and various household odds and ends. Ashley perused the selection of nail polishes, looking for a new shade.

"How about this lavender one?" suggested Christina, who favored all shades of purple.

"No, I want red—bright red." Ashley selected the brightest shade of red she could find and a pack of emery boards.

At the magazine rack, Christina pulled out a magazine about horoscopes.

"Don't you already know everything there is to know about that?" Ashley asked.

"Not everything," Christina said, thumbing through the magazine. "The planets are always changing. I want to know how they're aligned right now."

As Ashley waited, her eyes went wide at the sight of a headline in front of her. Christina glanced up and saw her expression. "What is it?" she asked, alarmed.

Ashley nodded toward a copy of *Tattletale*, a newspaper that specialized in celebrity stories—mostly false ones—and strange, oddball stories of freaky happenings.

Christina dropped her horoscope magazine. "Oh, no! Oh, no!"

At the top of the paper, a large red headline blared: *UFO Plants Miracle Herb!*

And Ashley's picture was right below it! She stood by the door in Dr. Jeffers's examining room, right next to the vase of angelbloom. Ashley knew exactly when the picture had been taken. She'd posed for Bill Peters the day he'd interviewed Dr. Jeffers. The vase and flowers just happened to be in the photo by coincidence.

Ashley plucked the newspaper from the rack. "'A miraculous, healing plant was recently found in the rural, hardscrabble town of Pine Ridge,'" she read.

"Hardscrabble?" Christina repeated.

Ashley looked up. "I think it means crummy."

"I wouldn't say that," Christina said, loyally indignant at the slight to her town.

"'The plant, known as angelbloom, was first found by a young monk in the mountains of Tibet,'" Ashley continued reading. "'The monk told *Tattletale* reporters who visited his mountain retreat that a huge ship "with many blinking lights," dispatched a shower of glowing green seeds onto the mountain.'"

"They're making that up!" Christina charged angrily.

Ashley nodded. "Probably." She continued reading. "'Petite, pretty, and vivacious Ashley Kingsley found the mysterious plant by her home in rural Pine Ridge.'" She stopped and smiled. "Petite, pretty and vivacious, what do you think of that?"

"Very nice, keep reading," Christina prodded.

"'When the flower began working miracle cures, Ashley brought it to the attention of a local veterinarian. This old-time country doctor is refusing to release the miraculous healing herb to the world, preferring to keep it for her private use. At this very moment, though, teams of scientists from pharmaceutical companies around the world are helicoptering into the Tibetan mountains in search of angelbloom—a gift to humanity from alien creatures from another planet.'"

"Oh, my gosh. Do you think that's true?" Christina asked, horrified. "Are all those helicopters going to Tibet?"

Ashley rolled the paper in her hands thoughtfully. "I have no idea," she said. It was hard to figure. Some of the article was true and some of it was wildly false, like the part about the UFO, for instance. And some of it was half true, like the part about Dr. Jeffers refusing to release the angelbloom to the world. The entire article was a mishmash of lies, truths, and half-truths.

"Everyone is going to read this," Christina wailed. "Where did they get this story?"

"Remember that guy John from the health food store?" Ashley said. "This is a lot like the story idea he and Bill Peters are working on for a movie script. He said they needed money. I'll bet the two of them sold the story and the photo to the *Tattletale* for the money."

"That makes sense," Christina agreed. "That has to be it. This is a disaster. A total disaster!"

Was it? Ashley wondered. Or was it the beginning of fame and wealth? Her picture was on the front page of *Tattletale*. It was happening already. She was becoming famous.

10

By Friday, the inn at the ranch was completely booked up for the weekend. Even though they didn't usually get busy until after school let out, the Kingsleys welcomed the business and scrambled to accommodate the rush, hiring temporary help and opening up the third floor of the bunkhouse.

Ashley wasn't sure if her parents realized it, but something was soon very clear to her. The people who came in booked trail rides, but they seemed more interested in meeting Ashley and seeing the Pine Manor woods than in riding.

Delighted with the attention, Ashley responded to their questions with carefully thought-out replies that she practiced in her bedroom mirror at night.

"No, I did not see a UFO."

"The first animal cured was Junior, our colt."

"No, I haven't been aboard a spaceship. I have no idea why they wrote that."

"No, I haven't been contacted by monks in Tibet. I

have no idea if that stuff about them is true or not."

And on and on. Ashley prided herself on answering the questions honestly. The only part she left out was about the angels. That part was too personal. She didn't want to share it. It would be like handing something very precious over to people she didn't even know.

Naturally, her parents had had questions about the article. They already knew about the angelbloom, of course. But she'd had to explain how the article came to be.

"Have you spoken to Dr. Jeffers since this story came out?" her mother had inquired anxiously that afternoon.

Ashley had shaken her head. She hadn't heard from Dr. Jeffers and she hadn't had the nerve to call her. Ashley hoped she wasn't angry about it. She certainly hoped Dr. Jeffers didn't think Ashley had given the story to *Tattletale.*

Several times she'd picked up the phone to call Dr. Jeffers, but put it down again, too chickenhearted to complete the call. "If Dr. J. was angry, she'd have phoned me by now," she'd said to herself as she hung up.

Or was Dr. Jeffers so furious she couldn't even speak to Ashley?

No, Ashley assured herself. *Why should she be angry? Her name hadn't even been mentioned in the article.*

Too nervous and excited to sleep that night, Ashley came out of her room around midnight, feeling thirsty for a glass of milk. She came to the kitchen and found her mother standing in front of the refrigerator, the freezer door open. Coming closer, Ashley saw she was holding the clear freezer bag containing the angelbloom, staring at it.

Ashley silently watched her mother until, sensing her presence, her mother turned and looked at her. "There's something more about this plant, isn't there?" she said quietly, not seeming at all surprised to find Ashley there. "There's something you're not telling us."

"The angels put it in the woods," Ashley blurted out, relieved to say the words. She wanted to tell her mother. It seemed important somehow.

Mrs. Kingsley nodded and looked back at the bag of angelbloom. She and Ashley had talked about the angels before. Doubtful at first, Mrs. Kingsley had finally come around to believing it was possible they existed. "This is a great gift, then," she said, still looking at the brownish, frozen flowers. She looked back at Ashley. "A great gift."

"I know," Ashley said.

"It seems like the angelbloom should be in a church, not in my freezer," Mrs. Kingsley said uneasily.

"I don't think the angels care," Ashley said, feeling confident she was right.

"Maybe not," Mrs. Kingsley agreed, returning the bag to the freezer. "Dr. Jeffers is a smart woman and a good person. I know she'll use this flower with respect. When I was growing up, she was the person I most admired."

Ashley came alongside her mother and opened the refrigerator door. "Really?"

"Yes," Mrs. Kingsley said. "She'd come by with her father and they'd take care of the horses. I wanted to be a veterinarian just like her."

Pouring herself some milk, Ashley gazed hard at her

mother. She'd never known this. "Why didn't you become one?"

"There was no money for college at the time, and my parents needed me at the ranch. Then I met your father, and we got married and took over the ranch. I just forgot about it, I suppose."

"I think I'd like to be a vet," Ashley confided.

Her mother looked surprised. Then a worried look settled over her face like a rain cloud.

"I'm working on getting a scholarship," Ashley said, understanding her mother's worried expression. "I'm doing a project on the angelbloom."

Mrs. Kingsley smiled softly. "College is a ways off. Our finances might improve by the time you graduate high school." She kissed the top of Ashley's hair and headed out of the kitchen. "Good-night."

"Good-night." Things *were* definitely going to improve, Ashley thought as she finished her milk. Her mother had no idea how much things were going to change. Ashley felt sure of it.

It seemed almost everyone had read the *Tattletale* story and wanted to know about angelbloom. The kids in school had been curious. Even her teachers had had questions for her.

"Is Dr. Jeffers the veterinarian who has the angelbloom?" Ms. Perez had guessed. "Tell her she must make the plant available to the world."

Ashley had squinted slightly at Ms. Perez, thinking. Even though her teacher was intelligent enough to know *Tattletale* was a trashy paper, she'd read it. And she seemed to believe some of it. Why else would she say Dr.

Jeffers had to make the plant available? *Tattletale* was the only place she could have read that Dr. Jeffers was holding it back.

"She needs to run more tests on the flower first," Ashley had said, feeling very wise and mature as she spoke.

"Yes, I suppose so," Ms. Perez had conceded. Then, she'd clutched Ashley's arm enthusiastically. "Ashley, this is such an opportunity for you. If the importance of this discovery is reflected in your project, I know you'll do very well with the judges. Make sure to cover all of Dr. Jeffers's tests. Has she done much yet?"

"Not yet."

"Don't let her delay," Ms. Perez had urged. She'd headed into the classroom, then stopped and turned back, speaking in a near whisper. "I assume the part about the UFOs was made up."

Ashley had nodded.

"I thought so," Ms. Perez had said with a wink and a somewhat relieved expression.

* * *

"I didn't give this story to them, honest," Ashley told Dr. Jeffers that Saturday when she went to her office. "It came from Bill Peters and a friend of his who works in the health food store. They're trying to write a script for a movie about it."

Dr. Jeffers nodded, frowning. "A movie, eh?" She pushed her desk chair back and folded her arms.

Ashley went on to explain again how Bill Peters had called while she was upstairs writing Dr. Jeffers the note. "Maybe I shouldn't have told him about the chipmunk, but I was so excited, I was just dying to tell someone."

Dr. Jeffers drummed her desk with her fingertips. "At least they didn't use my name. I'd take them to court if they had. How do you feel about them using your name and picture?"

"I don't mind. They said nice stuff about me, after all," Ashley replied.

"Yes, they did." Dr. Jeffers smiled, and Ashley exhaled with relief. When she'd first come in she wasn't sure if Dr. Jeffers was angry or not. It had seemed that Dr. Jeffers was still making up her mind about that herself. Now her smile told Ashley everything was all right.

"Were you totally blown away when you saw the chipmunk?" Ashley asked.

Dr. Jeffers pushed back her chair and stood. "It was quite exciting," she agreed. "I kept him for observation until yesterday. Then I had Clematis set him free."

"Lucky chipmunk," Ashley said as she followed Dr. Jeffers from the office to the examining room.

"What's up?" Too-too greeted them when they entered. Except for the iguana and Too-too, the Siamese cat was the only animal there.

Dr. Jeffers lifted her limp body from the cage and stroked her back, sighing. "All her tests came back negative. She doesn't have an infection, no parasites, her blood count is normal. I've been feeding her a vitamin-rich diet since she got here. I even gave her a little cod-liver oil the other day, hoping to cleanse her system. She drank it, but she isn't any better. I'm completely stumped."

"Give her some angelbloom," Ashley suggested enthusiastically.

"It's still too soon for that," Dr. Jeffers disagreed. "I ran a litmus test on it yesterday. And I want to test it for alkaline or acid components today."

"I don't understand," Ashley admitted.

"I want to see what its elements are. What it's made up of."

"What does it matter? It works," Ashley insisted.

Dr. Jeffers put Muffy on the table and checked her ears and eyes with her penlight. "It matters. Not all medicinal compounds work on all things. In fact, some might be contraindicated in some instances."

"Contra-what?" Ashley questioned.

"You shouldn't give it at all. It could be harmful," Dr. Jeffers explained, turning Muffy onto her back. "Or in other cases, it should be given only in tiny doses."

"Maybe you're being a little *too* careful," Ashley dared to suggest. She had to get Dr. Jeffers moving on this or she wouldn't have enough material for her project.

"I can't administer a cure without knowing its proper use," Dr. Jeffers countered. She glanced at a page of appointments that hung on her bulletin board. "I have to go out to check on John O'Herlihy's cow," she said. "She's not milking properly. Clematis will be here soon. Can you handle things till then?"

"Sure."

"If no one calls or drops in with an animal by two o'clock, just go home. I'll be out working with livestock most of the day, but I'll call you before two."

"No problem," Ashley agreed.

Dr. Jeffers went out the door, then stepped back in. "By the way. WPNE called this morning." WPNE was the local cable TV station. "They want to interview me tomorrow morning at eleven."

"Are you going to do it?" Ashley asked excitedly.

"Yes. Want to join me?"

"Me?"

"Yes, you."

"Awesome! Yes! Yes! I would love to come!" Ashley suddenly frowned. "I'm surprised you said yes."

"I want to set the record straight about angelbloom. This is my chance to dampen some of the curiosity and wild stories that are spreading. *Tattletale* can't write anything else if I tell the truth."

"That's true," Ashley said quietly. She didn't like the sound of this. Dr. Jeffers would go on TV and make the whole thing sound dull and scientific. No one would be interested in it after that.

"Bye," Dr. Jeffers said, leaving. "I'll pick you up for the interview tomorrow at ten, all right?"

"Great," Ashley said a bit absently. She was thinking about something else. Thinking hard.

Between today and tomorrow, something exciting had to happen with the angelbloom—something that Dr. Jeffers could talk about on TV. But what?

Ashley leaned her elbows on the examining table and propped her chin on them. She had to think of something.

A scuffling sound came from Muffy's cage as the cat shifted position. With a slow, sidelong glance, Ashley looked at the cat. "Muffy," she said softly.

Walking to the cage, Ashley knelt in front of it. The poor cat. Her blue eyes were listless, her coat so dull. She had to be unhappy. She certainly looked it.

The angelbloom would make her better.

It was really so simple. Ashley didn't know why Dr. Jeffers kept resisting the idea of giving it to Muffy. Sure, it was good to be careful, but she herself had said that she was stumped.

Muffy would probably just waste away and die eventually, if something wasn't done for her.

Ashley glanced over her shoulder at the vase of angelbloom on the table. Dr. Jeffers did not want the flower given to Muffy. She'd been completely clear on it. If Ashley gave Muffy the angelbloom, she'd be directly disobeying Dr. Jeffers's wishes. What if Dr. Jeffers was furious? What if she told Ashley never to come back?

But she wouldn't do those things. Not if the angelbloom worked.

And Ashley was sure it *would* work.

She got to her feet. *Sometimes a person just has to trust her own instincts*, she told herself as she crossed the room to the vase. *This is one of those times*.

None of the angelbloom in the vase had flowered, but there were several fat buds that looked as though they would burst open at any moment. Ashley snapped four of the fattest ones from their stems.

Moving fast now, letting action block out any misgivings, Ashley prepared the angelbloom tea. It took the water ages to boil. Ages! She paced anxiously as she waited. Finally a few bubbles formed on the sides of the pot. *Good enough*, Ashley thought.

Hands trembling, she worked her fingers into the fat, green buds. They didn't open easily. She felt as if they were almost fighting her prying intrusion.

"There!" she breathed as a bud, at last, gave way, revealing a fuzzy damp mix of purple and vivid pink petals. She pulled the petals apart and threw them into the now roiling, churning water. They spun in a circle, throwing off their pink and purple colors.

Ashley worked on the next bud even more feverishly. Within five minutes, all four buds were opened and in the pot. The water shimmered with purple bubbles. She recalled that the brew Dr. Jeffers had made was a lighter pink. *Because she didn't boil it as long*, Ashley decided as she turned off the gas and took the pot from the burner.

After straining the tea, Ashley brought it back to the examining room in a teacup. She blew on it, impatient for it to cool.

"Oh, boy. Big trouble!" Too-too cried. "What's up? Big trouble!"

"Be quiet," Ashley scolded. "Who asked you?" The cockatoo dipped his head and ruffled his crown.

Ashley took Muffy from the cage. Filling the eye-dropper with purple tea, Ashley pried Muffy's jaw open with her fingers at each side of the cat's mouth as she'd seen Dr. Jeffers do. Muffy was so droopy, she put up almost no resistance. "There you go," Ashley said sooth-ingly as she squeezed the contents of the eyedropper into Muffy's mouth. Just to be sure, Ashley gave Muffy two more eyedroppersful.

When she was finished, Ashley stood back and stared

at Muffy. The cat blinked her blue eyes and seemed about to go to sleep. Ashley heard someone opening the patio door.

Clematis!

Seized with guilt and panic, Ashley grabbed Muffy, tossed her into her cage, and fumbled the lock closed.

"Oh, boy! Big trouble!"

"Quiet!" she hissed at Too-too. The kitchen! She'd left the stems and half the tea in the kitchen. Clutching the kettle, she darted into the hall and saw Clematis about to go into Dr. Jeffers's office.

"Hi," Ashley said, her voice high and nervous. She wrapped her hands around the kettle in an effort to conceal it.

Behind her glasses, Clematis's eyes narrowed suspiciously. "Hello," she said. "Is everything all right?"

"Fine," Ashley said, working to lower and steady her voice. What was she upset about, anyway? She hadn't done anything bad. And who cared what Clematis thought? Dr. Jeffers would find out soon enough that the angelbloom had worked.

Still, Ashley couldn't stop her heart from pounding as she went to the kitchen to clean up. She washed out the kettle and the pot. Crumpling the remaining stems of angelbloom into as small a ball as she could, she buried them under some papers in the tall metal trash can. Why was she acting this way? she scolded herself. She was behaving like a criminal when she hadn't done anything wrong. All right, she'd disobeyed Dr. Jeffers, but what she'd done hadn't actually been bad.

As she stepped out of the kitchen, Ashley saw

Clematis cross the hall from the office to the examining room. She wished Clematis wasn't there. The woman made Ashley uneasy.

Ashley heard Clematis moving around in the examining room. Ashley had to go in to check on Muffy. She'd just ignore Clematis.

Stepping into the room, Ashley stopped short and stared.

Clematis held Muffy. The cat was wriggling in her arms. She squirmed free and stretched up to Clematis's shoulder. She licked Clematis's pale cheek.

"She's better!" Ashley gasped.

Clematis nodded. "It's like a miracle."

11

On Sunday morning, Ashley stood in front of her mirror and fluffed her curls with a hair pick. "Well, yes," she said, practicing her answer to an imaginary interviewer. "I knew a bold step was needed. Some might say it was rash to give the cat the angelbloom, but I felt confident. And, as you now know, Geraldo, it was the best thing I could possibly have done. Since then, angelbloom has wiped most major illnesses off the planet."

Ashley practiced laughing at the witty remarks the interviewer might make at that point and decided her laugh was too high and girlish. She tried a lower register and decided it sounded it better.

"What's next for me? Well, Geraldo, there's so much happening, I can hardly believe it. I'm receiving an honorary degree from Harvard, and then I'm off to accept the Nobel Peace Prize. I'll have to rush back to start filming my educational special, *The World of Herbal Healing.*"

Ashley laughed her own normal laugh. She knew she was being silly. But was she? Really? After all, she'd taken a risk and it had paid off. Paid off spectacularly. Muffy was completely cured—and Ashley had been the one to cure her!

When Dr. Jeffers had called just before two o'clock, Clematis had told her about Muffy. But Clematis hadn't known *why* the cat was better. Ashley hadn't told her. She wanted to be the one to tell Dr. Jeffers. She planned to do it this morning before they went in to be interviewed. "Isn't it great about Muffy?" she planned to say. "Guess what? I gave her the angelbloom and it worked."

Ashley could just picture Dr. Jeffers's face!

Shock. Amazement. Then gratitude and respect.

Once she knew the angelbloom had cured Muffy, Dr. Jeffers would want to charge full speed ahead on her research. Ashley just knew it.

Finishing her hair, Ashley selected a light green blouse with a wide collar and long, full sleeves that were gathered at the wrists. She put it on with a short blue skirt and her new chunky-heeled black shoes that made her a full inch taller. She was pleased with the effect: serious yet pretty.

Ashley went to the kitchen and found her mother taking a pot of boiling water off the stove.

"Ready for your big interview?" Mrs. Kingsley asked pleasantly as she poured some of the water into a teacup.

"I think so. I suppose I'm a little nervous."

"You'll be great. Listen, I'm taking a trail ride out with Dad. Jeremy and Jason went into town with Alice to get feed. Dr. Jeffers is coming to pick you up, right?"

"Right."

She kissed Ashley on the head. "Okay, then. Good luck."

"Thanks."

As her mother went out, carrying her tea with her, Ashley heard her say, "She's in the kitchen." In a moment, Christina, Molly, and Katie came in.

"Want to take out some horses and go for a ride?" Christina asked as she pulled out a kitchen chair and made herself at home.

"Can't. I'm going to be on TV with Dr. Jeffers."

"Cool!" Katie cried. "Why didn't you tell us?"

"I just found out yesterday." She told them about the upcoming interview and then about how she'd cured Muffy with the angelbloom.

"You didn't!" Molly cried. "Weren't you scared something might go wrong?"

"What could go wrong?" Ashley scoffed. "It worked on Junior and the chipmunk and it worked on Muffy. Angelbloom doesn't go wrong. Not ever. It's a gift from the angels. A miracle cure."

"You sound so sure," Christina said solemnly, frowning.

"I am sure," Ashley said. "Now that it's worked three times, I'm positive."

"Wow! Could I write a story about it for the school paper?" Katie asked.

"Not until next fall, okay?" Ashley said. "I don't want anyone jumping in and stealing my project. I'm going to start it today after the interview."

"But it's already been in the papers and you're going on TV," Katie objected.

As she spoke, the phone rang. "Hello?" Turning away from Katie, Ashley answered it.

"Hi, Ashley, this is Dr. Jeffers. The station just called me. They've had a scheduling problem and asked if we could get there an hour early."

Ashley checked the kitchen clock. "That's a half hour from now."

"I know. It's tight. Could you possibly get a lift? If I drive straight there, they'll be able to start filming the program on time even if you get there a little late."

"No problem," Ashley said. "Have you checked on Muffy?"

"Yes, it's unbelievable. Clematis said she just seemed to spring to life. Ms. Jameson has agreed to leave her another few days so I can watch her. I'd like to run some more tests on Muffy to see if her blood count or other test results changed in any way. But I shouldn't talk now. I'd better dash. I'll see you at the station. Do you know where it is?"

"Yes, I do. I'll see you there. Bye." She hung up and turned to her friends. "I've got to go ask someone to give me a . . ." She punched the air, frustrated. "No one's around! I forgot! I'll have to ride my bike."

Molly reached into the pocket of her black satin baseball jacket and took out her cellular phone. "Want me to call the limo service my dad uses?" she asked. "He has an account with them. You can just sign my name to pay for it."

"No, thanks," Ashley said, pulling off her shoes. "I can ride my bike and be there in a half hour."

"But you'll look all sweaty and gross," Molly objected.

Ashley considered it for a moment but decided to ride her bike. The idea of taking a limousine just seemed too weird right now. She knew where the studio was and it wasn't a bad ride. "Be right back," she said. She ran to her room and grabbed her white canvas sneakers from the closet. After putting them on and tossing her good shoes into her small knapsack, she ran back to the kitchen.

"What's the matter with Champ?" Katie asked as soon as Ashley stepped in.

"Nothing. What do you mean?" Ashley followed Katie's gaze over to the refrigerator where Champ lay sprawled on the floor.

"I think he puked up some grass," Christina said. "Look."

Sure enough. Near Champ was a small puddle of saliva with bits of grass in it.

"Don't dogs eat grass when they're getting sick?" Katie asked.

Ashley quickly wiped up the grassy spit with a paper towel, then squatted beside Champ. "What's wrong?" she asked, stroking his golden coat. He raised his head and let out a low, pitiful whine.

"Sounds like he's got a bellyache or something," Christina said, coming alongside Ashley.

Ashley jumped to her feet. "I know what will fix him up." She went to the stove and turned the flame on high under the pot of tea water her mother had left behind. Then she opened the freezer door and pulled out the bag of frozen angelbloom.

"You're giving him that?" Katie questioned. "Are you sure you should?"

"Why not?" Ashley asked as she confidently snapped buds from the cold plant.

"It's a miracle cure, not Mom's chicken soup," Katie said.

"How do you know?" Ashley countered as she hurriedly pried open the tight, frozen buds. "Aspirin was a great gift to humankind, and it's used for everyday things." She ripped the flower apart and tossed the cold, moist petals into the boiling water. Soon the water took on a purple tint. Ashley strained it into Champ's water bowl. "Drink this and you'll be better soon," she told him.

"I'm late. I've got to get out of here," Ashley said, grabbing her knapsack and hurrying from the kitchen with her friends trailing behind. Her three-speed bike leaned against the side of the house.

"Good luck," Christina called as Ashley began pedaling down the dirt road.

"Thanks," Ashley called over her shoulder. She rode down the drive past the grazing horses in the fields. When she reached the ranch's front gate, she turned left and biked down the curving two-lane road that led into Pine Ridge. The studio was about two miles past the town. She was probably going to be late, but Dr. Jeffers would be there. They wouldn't have to wait for Ashley.

Pedaling fast, she made it to Pine Ridge in good time. Since it was Sunday morning, there wasn't much traffic to navigate. It shouldn't take her too long to make it to the studio. Ashley had just made it out of town when her front wheel wobbled back and forth as if it had a rebellious life of its own. Braking abruptly, she skidded to a stop. Instantly, she saw the problem. "Just my luck," she muttered. Her front tire had gone flat.

Ashley got off the bike and inspected the tire. There didn't seem to be any puncture in it. There must be a slow leak. As she'd ridden through town, she'd noticed that the Pine Ridge Garage was closed. She knew their air pump was inside so it wouldn't do any good to go there. And there wasn't enough time to go all the way back home. Then Ashley recalled seeing an air pump in the cabinet of Dr. Jeffer's office kitchen. Walking her bike, it would only take her about ten minutes. Going there was her best bet.

The bike was difficult to walk. The front wheel shook back and forth as she pushed the handlebars. Her hair was moist with perspiration by the time she reached Dr. Jeffers's big brick house. Ashley didn't see Clematis's old bike. No one was there. She prayed the door would be open.

Walking the bike around to the patio, Ashley noticed a newly made garden. Fresh dirt shone inside a wooden frame next to the stone wall. Curious, Ashley stopped for a moment and bent to read the markers by each small mound of fresh dirt. She recognized Clematis's neat curved script. "Lavender. Chamomile. Sarsaparilla," she read. An herb garden. On the last marker, "Angelbloom" was written.

Sun poured onto the patch of dirt. Ashley wondered if the angelbloom would grow here. Maybe it would. She pictured the creek bank by the Angels Crossing Bridge and how the blooming plants were the ones in the patch of sunshine by the water.

Ashley tried the side door and sighed with relief as it opened. Hurrying down the hall, she quickly found the air pump. As she ran out of the kitchen, she heard Too-too in the examining room. "Oh boy! Big trouble! Oh boy!"

There was no time to check on him now. She started down the hall.

"Big trouble! Big trouble!"

Ashley stopped by the door. Maybe she'd better check on him. That crazy bird might have his head stuck between the bars of his cage or something like that. She ran back to the examining room. "What's the matter, Too-too?"

The bird in his cage ruffled his crown.

"What?" Ashley asked.

Everything was quiet. Too quiet. She looked around at the cages.

"Muffy!" she gasped. The cat's long body lay sprawled across the length of her cage. Springing to the cage, Ashley unlatched the door and pulled the animal out. Her body was warm, but Ashley saw no sign of life. "Muffy, wake up!" she cried urgently, jiggling the cat.

It was no use. She didn't move.

Muffy was dead.

12

Ashley staggered out to the patio feeling dazed. The perspiration on her forehead was cold, clammy. Her hands trembled. The poor cat. Dr. Jeffers must have been right, and the angelbloom had killed her—Ashley had killed her!

How had this happened? What could have gone wrong?

Ashley leaned heavily on the patio table, her mind reeling. Did Dr. Jeffers already know about Muffy? Would she write about it? Would she talk about it on TV? What would it mean for the future of angelbloom?

Ashley felt as if an iron band were tightening around her chest. She could barely breathe.

What should she do? What?

Think, she urged herself. *Don't panic. Think calmly.*

Wait! Dr. Jeffers didn't know Ashley gave Muffy the angelbloom. And neither did Clematis. No one knew except her friends. Thank goodness she hadn't told!

She felt terrible about Muffy. Guilty. Awful. But no one

knew it was her fault. Dr. Jeffers would think the sick cat got better for a little while, then had a relapse. Simple. There was no reason Muffy's death should affect anything.

The only way anyone would know about the angel-bloom would be if Ashley acted all freaked out about it.

She had to stay calm. Calm.

Ashley's stomach lurched and she felt a violent urge to throw up. Stumbling toward the wall, she put her hands on its cool stone and waited to be sick. Nothing happened. Her body heaved in dry, heavy gasps. Her head spinning, she sat, squashing a fern near the wall. Resting her head on the stone, she waited for the nausea and dizziness to pass.

In minutes, it did pass. When Ashley lifted her head, she realized her hand was in the dirt of the new garden. Without noticing, she'd been clutching the dirt where the angelbloom had been planted.

Ashley yanked her hand away as if the dirt were hot. Pulling herself up, she brushed the dirt off on the wall. She wanted every bit of it off her. In the process, one of her perfect gleaming red fingernails snapped. Unexpectedly, tears sprang to her eyes. "Don't be an idiot!" she scolded herself, brusquely wiping her wet eyes with the back of her hand. It wasn't the nail. That could be fixed. It was just that everything was going wrong. Falling apart.

If she didn't fix her bike and get to the station fast, she'd miss the interview entirely. She'd think about everything that had happened later. Right now, the most important thing was to get to the station.

Ashley quickly pumped air into her tire. She pressed it

hard and, luckily, the tire held the air. Good. She got on her bike and pedaled away from the house, feeling as if she were fleeing some terrible place.

Even when she could no longer see the house over her shoulder, Ashley felt like some terrible thing was chasing her. She pedaled even harder, but the bike didn't seem to go any faster. She clicked the speeds and the bike pedal loosened. It loosened too much and too quickly. Ashley skidded on some loose gravel and slid into a patch of prickly raspberry bushes.

With an enraged, frustrated scream, she pulled herself out of the bushes. She began struggling with the bike, which lay ensnared in the thorns.

As she fought with the handlebars, Ashley suddenly sensed a presence behind her. Whirling around, she found herself facing the chest of a uniformed police officer. His large motorcycle was parked a few feet away. She hadn't even heard it pull up. "Are you all right?" he asked.

Ashley wanted to cry. No, she wasn't all right. She was terrible!

She stared up at the officer. His dark skin glistened in the sunlight. His eyes were hidden behind impenetrable sunglasses, but his mouth smiled gently. "I'm not hurt," she replied. "At least not too bad. But my bike's stuck."

With unbelievable ease, the officer reached in and extricated the bike from the bush. He righted it in front of her. "That front tire has a slow leak," he said.

Ashley wondered how he knew. Newly pumped up, the tire looked fine right now.

"You should be wearing a helmet," he cautioned. He

went to his motorcycle and lifted the padded leather seat. Underneath was a storage compartment from which he pulled a gleaming black helmet. "Here," he said, offering it to her.

"Thank you," Ashley replied as she put it on her head. "How will I get it back to you?"

"Just keep it," he said. "Are you sure you're all right?"

"Yes." Strangely enough, Ashley did feel better. Perhaps it was just his kindness that made her feel so. "Thank you."

"Drive carefully and always wear your helmet," he said with a nod.

As the officer turned to go, the sun glanced off the nameplate on his chest. For a fleeting moment, Ashley wondered about him. She and her friends had met a police officer once whom Ned had told Katie was an angel. His name was Officer Winger. In fact, they'd met several officers with that same name.

Ashley stared at his back as he got on his motorcycle. With a wave of his leather-gloved hand, he drove away. She'd never know.

Ashley got back on her bike and began riding once again. Her body ached from her fall, but she was calmer now. She reached the station and saw Dr. Jeffers's red Jeep parked out front.

In the lobby, a receptionist directed Ashley to Studio A. Gently, she pushed on the heavy door and entered a quiet, darkened area. People stood around facing the center of the room where a brilliant spotlight shone on two people who sat on a bright blue couch talking— Dr. Jeffers and the show's host.

"Can I help you?" a man whispered to Ashley.

"I'm here for the show with Dr. Jeffers," she whispered back.

"Oh, you're the girl they've been worried about," the man said. Putting his hands on her shoulders, he guided her toward the brightly lit set. The host, a balding, heavy man in a gray suit, noticed their movement off-camera.

"I do believe Dr. Jeffers's assistant has finally arrived," he said with a wide, welcoming smile.

The man gave Ashley a slight push, urging her toward the host. Clutching her hands nervously, Ashley walked into the circle of light. "This is Ashley Kingsley, ladies and gentlemen," the host said in his super-friendly announcer's voice. "Those of you who saw the last issue of the infamous *Tattletale* will recognize this lovely young lady from the front page." He indicated that Ashley should sit on the couch between himself and Dr. Jeffers. "Ashley was the one who first brought angelbloom to your attention. Am I right about that, Dr. Jeffers?"

Dr. Jeffers smiled at Ashley. She looked pretty and younger than usual in a stylish red pantsuit. "Yes, that's right, Mike." She went on to tell the story of how Junior had eaten the angelbloom when Ashley unintentionally left a bouquet of it in his stall.

"Ashley," Mike said, "when you first picked the flower, did you sense something special about it?"

"Uh, no. I just thought it was pretty," Ashley answered honestly.

"But didn't something attract you to it—a certain . . . vibration, if you will?" Mike pressed.

Ashley thought again. The answer was still no. She'd

just liked the way the flowers had looked. But maybe that was too dull. From Mike's twinkling eyes and expectant expression, she sensed he'd be disappointed if she didn't say something interesting. "Well, I did sort of feel there was something special about the flowers," she lied. "There was kind of a little breeze around them, I guess."

"So, they more or less called to you in their own special way?"

"Yes." Dr. Jeffers looked at Ashley skeptically. "In a sort of way," Ashley amended quickly. "It was more like a feeling than a call."

Mike turned his gaze to Dr. Jeffers. "Did you have that same feeling when you first saw the angelbloom, Dr. Jeffers?"

"No. Not at all," Dr. Jeffers replied. "To me angelbloom is a plant. Like many other herbs, it seems to have healing properties. Granted, we've seen some spectacular results, but there are many variables to be considered. For example, I was giving Junior antibiotics at the time. The medicine might have simply taken hold at the same time the horse ate the angelbloom. The chipmunk I mentioned earlier might simply have been dazed by a fall. When I forced a liquid into him, it might have been all he needed to revive."

Mike blinked and turned back to Ashley. She could tell he hadn't liked Dr. Jeffers's too sensible reply. "Ashley, when you felt the breeze and vibrations around the angelbloom, did it occur to you that it might be from another planet?"

Dr. Jeffers pursed her lips and stared at Ashley, waiting for her answer. Mike looked at her brightly.

She wanted to please them both.

"Umm . . . yes and no," she said.

"Explain," Mike prodded, his eyes still bright, his expression eager.

"It was certainly possible that the angelbloom was from another planet, but there was no real reason for me to think so, except that anything is possible. I mean for all I know, you might be from another planet."

Mike frowned.

Ashley giggled nervously. "Or any of us might be! It's possible, right?" She felt foolish, like a ridiculous clown, but she couldn't help it. She was scared. She'd never been on TV before. She didn't know what to say.

"Of course. Of course," Mike said, regaining his smile. "I've certainly met a few space cadets in my day."

Ashley laughed politely. Dr. Jeffers didn't.

Mike's face grew earnest. "But seriously, Ashley, when did you first suspect the angelbloom was otherworldly?"

"When Junior got better," Ashley replied.

"I wouldn't say it was otherworldly," Dr. Jeffers interjected. "It's very much of this world, in fact. For centuries, plants have served humankind with their healing properties and although some, like angelbloom, are rare, it doesn't mean that..."

For Ashley, Dr. Jeffers's voice became a distant sound. Her attention had become completely fixed elsewhere.

Clematis had come into the studio. She stood just on the edge of the spotlight. The studio lamps were reflected in her glasses, the light bouncing off them like strange rays. Her pale face looked stern, almost angry.

In her arms, she cradled the dead cat.

13

"Excuse me," Dr. Jeffers said, abruptly getting up from the couch.

Mike looked alarmed at his guest's disappearance. He focused intently on Ashley. "Tell me about your work with Dr. Jeffers. How has this amazing woman influenced you?"

"Oh, she's great," Ashley murmured absently, her eyes riveted on Clematis and Dr. Jeffers. They stood close together, speaking urgently. Ashley couldn't stand it another second. She had to know what Clematis was saying. "Excuse me," she said, springing from the couch.

"Well, folks, that's the fast action life of a country veterinarian and her assistant," Mike said to the cameras.

Ashley's heart pounded in her chest with the ferocity and speed of a jackhammer. Her throat had dried to sandpaper. When she reached Clematis and Dr. Jeffers, she couldn't speak. She could only look at them with wide inquiring eyes.

"She's so much worse," Dr. Jeffers said, stroking Muffy. "I don't understand it."

Worse? Ashley swallowed hard. "You mean she's not dead?"

Clematis shook her head. "She's breathing."

Ashley reeled with relief. She staggered back, trying to regain her balance. Muffy wasn't dead. She was alive. That meant Dr. Jeffers might still be able to save her. Maybe Ashley hadn't killed her, after all.

Clematis peered at Ashley with accusing eyes. "She was lying on the table when I found her. Did you take her out of her cage?"

"No. No!" Ashley lied desperately. "I came straight to the studio."

"That's pretty odd, then," Clematis said, looking unblinkingly at Ashley.

Ashley was seized with a terrible desire to shove Clematis hard against the wall. Never before had she experienced such a violent dislike for someone. And now, more than ever, she wanted to push Clematis away, to see her bottle-thick glasses fly into the air, to see her hit the wall hard.

"Are you all right, Ashley?" Dr. Jeffers asked.

Ashley tried to reply, but she was choked with emotion—guilt, anger, fear. Her mouth opened and closed silently. Scalding tears rushed to her eyes. She had to get away! She couldn't stand to see the sick cat or Clematis. Even Dr. Jeffers's concern was too much.

Slamming her hands against the studio door, Ashley pushed it open and ran down the hall. "Ashley!" she heard Dr. Jeffers call, but she didn't turn back. Yanking her bike from the rack, she got on and pedaled madly, hardly even aware of where she was going. The black helmet she'd strapped to the handlebars banged against the metal when she bumped heedlessly over a low curb.

A car horn blared as she veered into the middle of the road. She pulled sharply off to the side just in time to miss hitting a blue station wagon. "Watch where you're going!" a teenage boy shouted at her from the open car window.

Ashley glanced back at the TV station just as Dr. Jeffers burst through the front door. Not wanting Dr. Jeffers to catch up with her, Ashley got back on her bike and began pedaling fast.

With her head down, she biked back into town. She spotted Jeremy and Jason coming out of the feed store. "Hey, Ashley," Jason called to her.

Ashley kept her head down, pretending she hadn't heard him. She didn't want to speak to anyone. What she needed right now was to be alone. All alone.

After another fifteen minutes of mad, mindless, desperate pedaling, Ashley's front wheel jerked sharply to the left. "Not again!" she shouted as the bike skidded in a circle, almost throwing her off onto the road. As she suspected, the front tire was once again flat.

Peering down the road, Ashley realized she wasn't that far from home. It would take her about a half hour to walk the bike back to the ranch. The day was growing warm. The idea of pushing her bike along the usually busy road wasn't appealing.

To her right, a thick pine forest swayed gently in the spring breeze. This was the part of Pine Manor woods that bordered the road. It would be faster if Ashley cut through the woods and had someone drive her back later to retrieve the bike.

Ashley leaned the bike against a thick pine several yards in from the road. Entering the forest, she felt its coolness. She stopped a moment, waiting for the calm serenity the woods always brought her.

Nothing happened. Ashley's heart still raced, and she felt agitated, uneasy. A twig snapped and she jumped.

None of this was her fault, Ashley thought as she stomped through the woods. She'd only wanted good things for everyone—for herself, for her family, for Dr. Jeffers, even for the stupid cat! She hadn't meant any harm.

Besides, the cat wasn't even dead, so who cared, anyway?

Ashley passed through a stand of shimmering white birches and stopped to get her bearings. There should be two waterfalls feeding into a natural pool nearby, she knew. She continued on, leaving the birches behind and entering dense pine woods again.

What happened to the waterfalls? she wondered. *They shouldn't have been far from the birches.*

She walked on and soon she wasn't sure where she was.

"Oh, great," Ashley muttered bitterly. "Now I'll have to go back." Turning, she was suddenly unsure which direction she'd come from. All the pines looked alike. There was no boulder, no ridge, no distinctive looking tree or plant she could remember passing.

Then Ashley became aware of the song of rushing

water, like a friend calling to her. "The creek!" she murmured. Running in the sound's direction, she finally saw the creek, cutting a shining crystal blue path through the dense green and brown woods.

She hurried along the water's edge, not sure why she was rushing. But something inside was driving her on as though she needed to reach a destination she wasn't yet sure of.

But when Ashley saw it, she was sure.

The Angels Crossing Bridge appeared sooner than she would have expected. It stood, spanning the creek like a welcoming home. Her heart leaped unreasonably at the sight of it, and she began running full out toward it.

But when Ashley reached the bridge, she stopped. On the bank of the creek, rows of angelbloom stood, their open pink-purple blossoms a wave of brilliant color. She noticed that the blossoms appeared only in the patches of sunlight glinting through the trees, forming a pink-purple map of the sun's pattern. Those in wavering sunlight were smaller. The buds of those in shade were still shut tight.

Ashley stared at the angelbloom.

The hateful, treacherous plant.

It had built up her hopes only to betray her. Why had it turned on her? Why had it hurt the cat?

It had hurt her, too.

It had dashed her hopes, but it had also done her worse harm, she thought angrily. She saw herself on the TV show, giggling like an idiot, saying stupid things. She could barely recognize that girl. It had turned her into a liar, too. She'd lied on TV, lied to Dr. Jeffers.

And worse, she'd lied to herself. She'd thought she could be a veterinarian, somebody important—someone rich and famous. Ha! What a laugh. She'd never be any of those things.

Once—before discovering the angelbloom—seeing her future as working on the ranch had been enough. But it wasn't enough anymore. Because of the angelbloom, she'd dared to dream of having more, and now that she'd dreamed it, hoped for it, felt sure it was within her grasp, she didn't want to settle for less.

Only, now she'd have to.

The angelbloom was like a thief. It had robbed her of her dreams.

Ashley sat on the ground. She felt exhausted. Tears rolled down her cheeks. Burying her face in her hands, she let the tears fall freely. "Please," she murmured. "I feel so awful inside. I'm so confused. I don't know what to do."

The sound of footsteps on the bridge made her look up sharply. A female form was moving across the bridge, but the sunlight glancing off the bridge's roof blinded Ashley. She couldn't see the person clearly.

A flame of hope shot up inside her. Was it an angel? Had an angel come to show her what to do?

"Ashley?" Christina stepped from the bridge. "What are you doing here?"

With a rough swipe at her eyes, Ashley dried them. "I was . . . uh . . . I was riding home and my tire went flat so I thought I'd cut through the woods to get home faster."

Christina scrutinized her with a worried expression. "Are you all right?"

"Yeah, sure."

"You've been crying."

Ashley kicked a stick lying at her feet. "I don't know. I was just thinking about some things. Why are you here?"

"I was looking for Champ."

"Champ?"

"Nobody's seen him since you left, and I thought maybe he was in the woods."

Ashley suddenly started to tremble. She felt as if the blood were draining out of her body.

"Ashley, what's wrong?" Christina demanded, taking her friend's arm.

"Champ!" Ashley gasped. "I gave him the angelbloom!"

"So?"

Ashley broke free of Christina's grasp and began running across the bridge. "So, we have to find him," she said. "We have to find him fast."

14

Ashley stood in the stable doorway, panting heavily. She'd run all the way back from the bridge with Christina at her side. "He's not here," she gasped. "He's not in his bed."

"I told you nobody's seen him. I already checked here." Christina leaned against the doorway to rest. She puffed hard and swatted back a strand of hair wet with perspiration. "Why are you so worried about him taking the angelbloom?" she asked breathlessly.

Ashley clasped Christina's arm. "You can't tell anybody what I'm about to say. Swear."

"I swear."

"I gave the cat in Dr. Jeffers's office the angelbloom tea and she almost died. She might still die if Dr. Jeffers can't save her."

Shocked, Christina covered her gaping mouth with one hand.

Ashley hated the look on her face, so stunned and horrified. "I thought it was safe," she said in a small voice.

"Oh, no," Christina said, putting her hand over her heart. " Ashley, you've got to tell Dr. Jeffers what you've done. If she knows, then maybe she can find a cure."

"I can't tell her," Ashley insisted, turning away.

"Why not?"

Ashley whirled around to face her. "Because I knew she didn't want to give the cat the angelbloom, but I did it, anyway. I thought I was right and she was wrong. She'll be furious if she finds out. That cat cost a fortune. Her owner is going to freak if she dies. Dr. Jeffers will never trust me again, let alone have me work there anymore."

"Ashley," Christina said softly, "you can't lie about—"

"You swore you wouldn't tell," Ashley whispered ferociously.

"I won't, but, Ashley, this isn't like you at all. You're not a liar. You *have* to tell her."

Ashley just shook her head. No, she wasn't a liar. But this was worse than anything she'd ever had to deal with before. She couldn't do the right thing. The right thing was too hard. "I can't think about this now," Ashley said, walking into the stable just to get away from Christina. "I have to find Champ. That's the only thing I can think about right now."

Jeremy came into the stable. "Champ's not here?" he asked casually. He had no way of knowing why it was so important to find the dog.

"He's not in his bed," Ashley answered, "and he's not in the woods. I haven't looked anywhere else, though."

"He didn't eat any of the food in his dish, which is weird, and he threw up some grass on the porch," Jeremy said as he unhurriedly checked the horse stalls.

Occasionally, Champ paid one of the horses a visit and bedded down in a stall for a nap. "I was just worried that maybe he was sick or something."

"I'm worried, too," Ashley said, joining him in checking the stalls. "He always hangs around. He never wanders off."

"And he *always* eats his food," Jeremy said, chuckling.

Christina started checking the stalls at the far side of the stable. One by one, Ashley checked the row of stalls down to the large stall at the end where Bridey was still stabled with her filly. The little horse turned away from her nursing when Ashley stepped in and gazed at her. Ashley smiled, remembering how she'd felt when the filly was born—like she was at the center of all life. How had she come so far away from that feeling in such a short time?

A patch of gold fur in the hay on the far side of the stall caught her eye. "Champ!" Ashley cried, rushing to where he lay half buried in hay as if he'd burrowed his way into the stack.

The retriever's golden brown eyes were half-closed. His breathing was labored and heavy. A low wheeze rumbled up from his chest. "Christina! Jeremy!" she shouted. "Come quick!"

In seconds, Christina and Jeremy burst into the stall. "He looks bad," Jeremy cried, alarmed.

"Get Mom and Dad," Ashley said, brushing hay from Champ's coat.

"They're not here. After their trail ride, they drove into town to see a guy about boarding a horse here. I don't know exactly where they went."

"I'll get my mother," Christina suggested, already halfway out of the stall.

"She and Jason are out with a group on a trail ride," Jeremy reported. "Let's take him to Dr. Jeffers's. I'll drive Jason's car."

After the way she'd behaved at the studio, Ashley didn't want to see Dr. Jeffers. But she'd have to face her sooner or later if she wanted to keep her job. Besides, this was an emergency.

It took both Jeremy and Ashley to lift Champ, who listlessly submitted to being carried. Christina cleared a path, opening doors and moving objects out of the way. Struggling under his weight, they carried him to Jason's old brown car and managed to get him into the back seat.

As they were closing the car door, Katie and Molly came around the side of the house. "Did you find him?" Katie asked.

"He's really sick," Christina reported. "We're taking him to see Dr. Jeffers."

Molly, Katie, and Christina squeezed into the backseat with Champ. Ashley got in front with Jeremy. Within minutes, they were driving away from the ranch. When they arrived at Dr. Jeffers's place, Ashley was relieved to see her Jeep parked in front.

Jeremy parked, jumped out, and, with Molly, Katie, and Christina's help, pulled Champ out of the car. "Are you coming or what?" he demanded of Ashley who hadn't moved from the front seat.

"Yes, uh-huh," she stammered, climbing out. She didn't want to go in, but she had to. She ran ahead of Jeremy and Christina to open the door for them.

Dr. Jeffers was in the hall when they entered, carrying Champ. "What's happening?" she asked urgently.

"It's Champ. He's real sick," Jeremy said. "We don't know what's wrong."

Christina caught Ashley's eye and looked at her meaningfully. Ashley turned away.

"Bring him into the examining room," Dr. Jeffers told them.

They laid him out on the table in the middle of the room. "When did he first seem sick?" Dr. Jeffers asked Ashley.

Ashley couldn't speak. Her mind was racing to figure out how she could tell the story without mentioning the angelbloom.

"This morning," Christina spoke for her. "He was sort of droopy and he spit up some grass."

"Besides grass, did he eat anything strange that you know of?" Dr. Jeffers inquired, carefully thumping Champ's side with her fingers.

Again, Christina peered pointedly at Ashley.

"Didn't you give him that stuff?" Molly said. "You know, the—"

"No!" Ashley interrupted her. "He didn't eat anything strange at all."

As she spoke, Champ began to shake, his entire body trembling violently.

"What's happening?" Ashley demanded, terrified.

"He's convulsing!" Dr. Jeffers said, her eyes riveted on Champ. "Clematis! Clematis!"

When Clematis didn't appear, Dr. Jeffers turned to Ashley. "Get Clematis for me. I need her. Everyone else, please get out."

"Will he be all right?" Ashley asked.

"I hope so. Muffy convulsed like this just an hour ago. Get Clematis."

Ashley glanced at Muffy lying limply in her cage. She couldn't tell if the cat was sleeping or dead.

Clematis rushed in and sized up the situation immediately. "Everyone out," she demanded, ushering them all out of the room.

Ashley stood in the doorway, looking at Champ. His body was still rocking up and down, thumping the table. He couldn't die. *He can't die*, she thought, *he just can't.*

Clematis saw her standing there and closed the door.

15

The four girls and Jeremy stood outside, leaning on the car. Waiting.

"What's taking so long?" Jeremy grumbled.

"Ashley, why didn't you let me tell her about giving Champ the angelbloom?" Molly asked.

"The what?" Jeremy asked, staring at Ashley.

"The flower Ashley found that Dr. Jeffers has been testing," Katie explained. "Yeah, why didn't you tell her?"

Ashley hated the way they were all looking at her. "Because it's not important," she answered defensively. "It's just a flower."

"You fed Champ a flower?" Jeremy asked.

"Ashley, you have to tell her," Christina urged. "You heard what she said about Muffy. And Champ's doing the same thing. It has to be the angelbloom."

"I don't have to tell anything!" Ashley exploded.

"What's going on?" Jeremy asked impatiently.

"Nothing!" Ashley shouted. "Nothing!" Feeling cornered, she turned and stormed away from them, crossing the road and walking into a field of high grass and wildflowers.

Looking over her shoulder, Ashley was both surprised and relieved that they didn't come after her. She couldn't stand listening to their accusations for another minute. It was unbearable. Who did they think they were? They acted so superior! They weren't in her shoes. They hadn't done the awful things she had. They didn't have to face up to it. Sure it was easy to say what she should do. They weren't her!

They were excited about nothing, anyway! Dr. Jeffers would find a way to cure Champ. She was the best vet in the area. Nothing would happen to him.

But what if it did? Ashley had had Champ since he was a puppy. He couldn't die now. He just couldn't.

She went down a gentle slope in the field. Lacy white wildflowers bloomed in knee-high drifts across her path. As she continued on, the flowers grew taller, reaching her waist. With her head down, she walked further into the field of flowers.

When she finally looked up, Ashley saw she'd come to a wide pond. Round green waterlily leaves floated on its still, blue-black surface, covering nearly a quarter of the water.

A bluish mist hovered just above the pond.

Ashley stopped and stared at the mist. How strange that it didn't appear anywhere else.

For some reason, she couldn't take her eyes off it. The way the mist slowly and silently swirled was mesmerizing.

As it shifted, Ashley thought she saw forms begin to take shape within it. She couldn't be positive. Perhaps it was only her imagination, the same as when she saw pictures in the clouds.

The mist kept moving. The shapes kept building.

Angels. Inside the mist were the bluish white forms of three tall, winged angels.

There was no longer any doubt in Ashley's mind. Wanting to get closer to them, Ashley absently kicked off her sneakers. In her stocking feet, she waded into the pond. The water was surprisingly warm as it washed around her bare legs.

The hem of her short skirt grew wet, but she waded in even further. It was as if the misty angels were drawing her to them. Yet, no matter how much closer Ashley got, their forms remained indistinct. She couldn't make out the features of their faces or any markings on their clothing.

At last Ashley came so close that it seemed she could touch them. She reached out and her hand passed through warm mist. Another step and she was inside the mist.

She'd passed through the angels, into them. And then she couldn't see them anymore. Instead, she was surrounded by a wall of misty white. She had the sensation that she had stepped right into the middle of a cloud.

In a minute, Ashley became aware of voices. Looking up, she saw images moving within the mist. They were people, small but with depth, like holograms. Breathing in sharply, Ashley realized that she could see herself among the other people in the mist. She could hear her own voice speaking, too.

As she focused on one particular group of people their

voices became more distinct, easier to distinguish from the other voices around her.

Ashley saw herself, only older, in her twenties. She wore a great leather pants outfit and she was stepping into a limo. Inside the limo, she picked up a car phone. "Tell my agent I'll be late for the radio show. That stupid poodle ruined my makeup while I was filming my TV special."

Ashley could hardly believe it. This must be her future! Looking around, she saw scenes from her life. There she was on her first day of kindergarten in Mrs. Muller's class. And there she was learning to ride in the corral. This *was* her life.

The scene she'd just witnessed *had* to be her future. She *would* be rich and famous, after all. Ashley wanted to see more.

Turning in a circle, she scanned the scenes until she once again found herself as an adult. It was amazing how much she looked like her mother, only she wore better clothes. Much better clothes.

Ashley gazed at a scene in which she wore a shimmering silver strapless gown. She was on a stage receiving some sort of award. "I'd like to thank all those who worked with me on my TV special, "Animals! Animals!" They deserve this Emmy, too."

Ashley smiled with delight. This was everything she'd ever dreamed of—more! And it was really going to happen!

The scene continued as the grown-up Ashley left the stage. In a hallway, fans clamored for her autograph. Then she spoke to a well-dressed man. "No. Tell the

Animal Defense Fund I won't appear at their boring old supper unless they pay me four times what they've offered. I'm a busy woman and I've just won an Emmy," she said. "As of tonight, my speaking fees have quadrupled."

Turning again, Ashley found another scene. She was older here, in her thirties. She looked pretty, but her face had a tired, angry expression. In a luxurious office with white leather furniture, she talked into a white phone.

"No, tell Christina Kramer I'm not in. I don't have time to talk to her," this older Ashley said in a harsh, unpleasant voice. "I don't care if she insists. She can't do anything for my career. I can't bother with her anymore." Ashley was stunned—and even more so when she saw her grown-up self light a cigarette and pour herself a glass of brandy. She gulped the drink, then poured another. Her phone rang again and she snapped it up. "I don't have time, I told you. I don't care who's calling. Tell them I'm not here."

She wouldn't be like that as an adult, would she? No. She'd never treat Christina that way. And why was she drinking so much, and smoking? She looked so unhappy. Was that why? It seemed as though she'd turned into a very nasty person.

Not liking this scene at all, Ashley turned away. She saw herself as a child once again. It was Christmas. Her father was handing her a puppy with a big red bow around his neck. Champ. She was cuddling him, overwhelmed with joy.

Poor Champ. What had she done to him?

Ashley didn't want to see anymore. She didn't like this.

It was just a trick. The angels were playing a trick to make her feel bad.

Well, she wasn't going to fall for it!

Pushing through the clouds of mist, Ashley cleared a path out of the haze. The force of her swinging arms dispersed the mist in all directions. What kind of crazy pond was this? She wanted out!

Hurrying, Ashley headed for land. She couldn't get out of there fast enough!

As she sloshed through the water, she stepped on a large, slimy rock. "Ahh!" she shouted as her foot slipped out from under her. Instinctively swallowing a mouthful of air, Ashley plunged beneath the surface of the water. She felt cool, soft lily pads brush her skin as she fell.

Ashley opened her eyes underwater. It was murky, brown. A line of air bubbles escaped her mouth, and she pressed her lips together to keep the rest in. What was this awful slimy stuff wavering all around her? Weeds of some sort? Vines?

Waterlilies. The long, tough stems of the leaves that floated on top of the water.

Ashley tried to swim up, but she couldn't. The slippery stems held her in their dense, viny grip. She'd become entangled in them.

They're only plants, she thought, trying to yank herself free. They wouldn't let go. Aghast at their surprising strength, Ashley struggled even harder to pull away. It seemed the harder she fought, the more hopelessly entangled she became.

A wide line of bubbles escaped from Ashley's mouth. Her red curls floated in front of her face like yet another diabolical water plant, making it impossible for her to see. Her lungs began to hurt, aching to release the air they held.

What was going on? Blindly, Ashley tore at the plants. Some ripped loose under her frantic attack, but there were more—wrapping around her ankles, around her arms. Panicking, Ashley began to think the plants were deliberately grabbing at her, murderously trying to pull her down to the murky bottom.

"Help!" she cried, but the sound was drowned in a surge of bubbles. Desperate, Ashley tried to call back the word. Warm, muddy pond water rushed into her open mouth.

Bolts of neon color zigzagged before her eyes.

Then everything disappeared.

16

Ashley's eyes slowly blinked open. She had no idea where she was. Feeling fuzzy and confused, she struggled up so that she was leaning on her elbows. She was on a cot outdoors next to a red barn, and there were animals all around her.

Nearby was a corral with small Shetland ponies. A bunny hutch stood by the end of her cot. A large white rabbit hopped out of its open wire-mesh door and went on its way, hopping into some berry-laden bushes near the corral.

Three black baby lambs strolled past, gazing at Ashley with mild curiosity. One stopped to *baaa* at her.

A fluttering sound distracted her. She looked up to see a parrot flying by in a blaze of flapping red wings. A family of quails passed her, the babies lined up neatly behind their mother, their little heads bobbing in time with hers.

Where am I? Ashley wondered.

Blinking hard, she peered around. How had she gotten

here? She worked hard to remember, but the last thing she could recall was struggling with the waterlilies in the strange pond.

She bolted forward, eyes wide, as an alarming idea came to her.

Was she dead?

But this was a farm of some sort. Ashley had never heard of a single religion where people thought they went to a farm after they died.

A woman with long black hair, wearing farmer's overalls, came around the side of the barn, holding a seal point Siamese cat in her arms. It was Norma! Was she carrying Muffy?

"How are you feeling?" Norma asked.

"All right, I guess," Ashley said. "Where am I?"

"You're in between," Norma replied.

Blonde, beautiful Edwina came out of the barn, wearing a long, straight gingham-checked dress with a white medical jacket over it. Champ trailed her.

"Champ!" Ashley cried. Her dog looked fine. Not sick at all. Ashley's frantic eyes darted between Edwina and Norma. "Am I dreaming?" Ashley demanded.

Edwina smiled. "Merrily, merrily, merrily, merrily, life is but a dream," she sang.

A noise from the direction of the barn made Ashley turn away from Edwina. Ned, also in overalls, his long, sandy hair tied back, came around the corner, holding an enormous armful of angelbloom. "Come and get it!" he shouted as he tossed the purple and pink blossoms onto the ground.

From all over, animals came hurrying to eat the

flower. Muffy leaped from Norma's arms and went to nibble the flowers. Champ left Edwina's side.

"No!" Ashley cried. "Champ, no!" She lunged forward to stop him, but a wave of dizziness threw her back. She closed her eyes and held her head. When the spinning subsided, she opened them again.

But now a blinding, awesome white light flooded her vision. Squinting, Ashley was finally able to focus.

Three angels with wings and halos and flowing, silver-white robes moved among the animals, feeding them the angelbloom.

"It's poisonous," Ashley murmured. "Why are you giving it to them? You can't. It's poisonous."

Edwina turned to her. "Greed is poisonous," she said softly as a baby lamb munched angelbloom from her hand.

Ned offered the long-stemmed flower to a black pony. "Everything comes in its time, Ashley," he said, smiling. "You can't rush the seasons. You can't rush yourself. You'll unfold just like these flowers. Don't be in such a rush."

"What do you mean?" Ashley asked. They went back to feeding the animals as if they hadn't heard her. *Don't rush.* Where had she heard that before?

It was back at the creek.

Edwina had said it about the angelbloom.

But what did it mean? Ashley still didn't know. Why didn't they just come out and explain?

"Because then you won't really know the answer," Norma spoke to her unasked question.

Ashley felt confused. What answer? How would she

know it if they didn't tell her? And what were they doing to these animals? Were they trying to kill them or heal them?

But they were angels! They *had* to know what they were doing. Yet why would they feed the animals angelbloom when it had made Muffy and Champ so sick?

Ashley watched in horror as Champ ate ravenously, devouring flower after flower. She had to stop him or it would kill him. Wouldn't it?

And what were Muffy and Champ even doing here? Were they in between, too? Not alive, yet not dead?

"I'm coming, Champ," she whispered, determined to reach her dog no matter what it took. Summoning all her willpower, Ashley hoisted herself from the cot and threw herself forward. She should have landed on the ground, but, instead, she kept falling as the ground seemed to melt beneath her. It was impossible to get hold of anything. Everything was spinning. She couldn't see the angels or the farm or the animals anymore. Just murky, spinning blackness.

With exploding lungs, Ashley shot out of the water.

Swallowing great gulps of air, she slowly realized that she was back in the pond.

She wasn't dead! Or even in between!

She was alive!

Moving as fast as she could, Ashley slogged out of the pond and threw herself onto the ground. Breathing heavily, she waited for her head to clear.

The mist was gone from the water. Around her, lacy white flowers waved gently in the breeze. She heard the hum of bees. Overhead, fat white clouds drifted lazily in the blue sky. Everything was normal. Nothing had changed.

But something *felt* different. Something inside.

She was different. It was hard to say exactly how, but Ashley sensed it. She felt calmer, whole again.

The feeling that had dogged her lately, the feeling that something was chasing her, something she couldn't escape . . . it was gone. Her heart no longer raced. The feeling of constant uneasiness, the restlessness—it was all gone. Ashley felt as if she'd reached some safe place within herself.

And she suddenly understood what that bad feeling had been.

Her own guilty conscience had been trailing her like some shadowy spirit. No wonder she could never escape. A person couldn't escape herself.

With a jolt, Ashley understood that she hadn't liked the person she'd started to become. Her ambition had begun to turn her into someone else. She'd forgotten about the really important things—honesty, loyalty, integrity— because she'd wanted so much to be rich and famous.

Sure, it was okay to want things. But it wasn't okay to be untrue to yourself to get them.

That's what she'd been doing. She'd been thinking only about what the angelbloom could get her, not about the good it could do if it was used properly. She'd even been willing to lie and cheat to get what she wanted.

Finally, she understood the harm she'd been doing herself—and others, too.

Ashley clambered to her knees, driven by the force of the idea that had just struck her. It flooded her mind with a picture of the angelbloom bouquet in Dr. Jeffers's office. The answer had been right there in front of her all along. How blind she'd been not to see it!

Don't rush.

She knew what it meant! Of course! Of course!

Ashley jumped to her feet and started running.

17

Breathless, Ashley crossed the road to her friends, who were still waiting by the car. Molly and Katie sat on the hood. Jeremy was sitting in the front seat, listening to the car radio. Christina stood, intently laying down cards of some kind on the roof of the car. When they saw Ashley coming toward them, their faces grew alarmed.

"What happened to you?" Katie asked, running to her.

Ashley realized that she was wet. Her hair hung in clumps. A stringy waterlily stem still clung to her mud-streaked shirt.

"I fell into a pond," she answered quickly, "but I'm okay. Any word on Champ?"

"Nothing yet," Jeremy told her. "How did you fall into a pond?"

"I can't explain now."

"Ashley, I'm doing a Native American medicine card reading for you," Christina said. "You won't believe the cards that are turning up."

"I can't look now," Ashley said. "I'll be back." She hurried around to the office door and went inside. Going straight to the examining room, she found Clematis and Dr. Jeffers standing over Champ, who lay without moving on the table.

Ashley paled and staggered back. Was she too late?

"He's still alive," Dr. Jeffers told her. "I gave him an injection a while ago to stop the convulsions. I still don't know what's wrong with him, though."

"He needs angelbloom," Ashley said.

"Ashley, I don't know if this case warrants it," Dr. Jeffers objected. She narrowed her eyes at Ashley. "What happened to you?"

"Nothing—everything—I don't know. I'm fine. Champ needs the angelbloom now. Really. Please."

"Maybe she's right," Clematis said knowingly. "Go on, Ashley. Tell Dr. Jeffers what you mean."

Dr. Jeffers looked at Clematis with surprise as Ashley continued. "You see, I already gave him angelbloom," Ashley admitted. "I gave some to Muffy, too."

"Ashley! You didn't!" Dr. Jeffers gasped.

"I did. Only I didn't use the flowers to make the tea. I ripped open the buds, but it doesn't work when you use buds. You have to use the flowers. You can't rush it. You have to give the animals the *flowers* to cure them."

"How do you know?" Dr. Jeffers asked doubtfully.

"Because it worked on Junior and the chipmunk, remember?" Ashley said. She turned to the vase and saw that three new flowers had opened. "Please let me try it on him," she pleaded.

"I think you should," Clematis told Dr. Jeffers.

"All right," Dr. Jeffers sighed. "All right. I don't know what else to do."

Ashley plucked the flowers and ran into the kitchen with them. As she threw the flowers into her pot of boiling water, she saw that they colored the water pink, not purple like the teas she'd given to Muffy and Champ. She should have seen it then, but she hadn't wanted to see. Tossing in ice cubes to cool the tea, Ashley poured it into the teapot.

She returned to the examining room with the teapot. Champ had revived a bit. He lifted his head as she came in and let out a low, pathetic whine. Ashley petted him between the ears. "You're going to be all right," she told him. Then, without waiting for a dish or an eyedropper, she poured the angelbloom tea right into his mouth from the spout.

Somehow Champ seemed to sense that the tea was good for him. He lapped it up as it ran out the sides of his mouth and onto the table.

"Save some for Muffy," Clematis reminded her.

"Let's see if it works on Champ first," Dr. Jeffers cautioned.

"It's going to work," Clematis said in a soft, confident voice.

Ashley looked at her and, for the first time, felt as if she really saw Clematis. Behind the rimless glasses and frazzled hair was a lovely gentle face filled with caring. Why hadn't Ashley noticed this before?

Champ lay his head down on the table and shut his eyes.

Ashley felt as if her heart screeched to a stop. Had she killed him?

She'd been so sure the angelbloom flowers would work.

"How's it going?" Jeremy asked from the doorway. Katie, Molly, and Christina were with him.

Christina rushed to Ashley's side. "You look about to faint," she observed with concern. "You'd better sit down."

Ashley shook her head and held Christina's arm tight. Leaning into Christina's shoulder, she began to cry. She'd been so sure. So sure.

Christina held her tightly. Molly and Katie came to her other side. Molly placed her hand on Ashley's back. "Don't cry," Katie said quietly.

But Ashley couldn't stop.

Then a long, low whine made Ashley pick up her head. "Champ!" she cried. His eyes were open. His head was up and his tail thumped the table.

Ashley threw her arms around her pet. "Champ!"

In the course of the next half hour, Champ showed strong signs of recovery. He got off his side and lay with his forelegs in front of him the way he usually did. The brightness returned to his eyes and the thump of his tail grew ever stronger and more restless.

"I'm going to give some to Muffy," Dr. Jeffers said.

But in her haste, Ashley had spilled the rest of the tea. "Those were the only flowers," she said apologetically.

"No, they weren't," Katie said. "Look."

Miraculously, two more of the buds in the vase had burst into bloom.

"Things come to us as we need them," Clematis commented, snapping off the flowers and handing them to Dr. Jeffers.

In minutes, Dr. Jeffers brewed more tea and fed it to the listless cat. In another half hour, she, too, showed definite signs of improvement, purring and licking her paws.

Ashley noticed that Clematis was no longer in the room. As everyone crowded around Champ, marveling at his condition, which improved by the minute, Ashley silently stole away in search of Clematis. She felt she owed her an apology—or *something*.

Ashley checked Dr. Jeffers's office. It was empty. She went outside to the patio. The moment she opened the door, a blast of afternoon sunlight hit her full in the face, momentarily blinding her.

When her eyes had adjusted somewhat, Ashley stood still in the doorway, stunned by the sight in front of her.

Bending over Dr. Jeffers's herb garden was a glorious angel in an emerald-green robe. Small blue flowers shone in her lustrous dark curls, illuminated by the sun-bright halo around her head. The angel seemed to be tending the garden.

Ashley blinked twice. When she looked again, the angel had disappeared.

And there was Clematis, kneeling by the garden.

She sensed Ashley's presence and turned to her, smiling. "I don't think the angelbloom will grow in this garden," she said. "It's too wild and mysterious to be tamed. Some things are. But the other herbs will do well here, and they have a beauty and power all their own. How's Champ?"

"He's going to get better," Ashley said in a small voice, still stunned to discover Clematis was an angel.

She was an angel, wasn't she? Or had it just been the sun in Ashley's eyes that had made her seem to glow?

No, Ashley had seen her. She'd had wings.

Hadn't she?

Clematis stood and brushed dirt from her frumpy looking dress. "I'm happy Champ will be feeling better soon. So will you," she said, pushing her glasses back up on the bridge of her nose. Speechless, Ashley watched as she walked out of the patio area, took her bike from the side of the house, and rode away.

* * *

Ashley, Jeremy, and Christina dropped Molly and Katie off and returned to the ranch with Champ just as the sun was beginning to set. The orange sun glinted off the windshield. Ashley peered through it and saw her parents standing in front of the house, talking to a tall man in a blue suit whom she didn't recognize.

"Where have you been?" Mrs. Kingsley asked as they got out of the car. "I've been calling everywhere."

"Sorry, Mom," Ashley said. "Champ got sick and we had to rush him to Dr. Jeffers's."

Mrs. Kingsley stared at Champ as he trotted up to the porch. "He looks fine now."

"The angelbloom cured him," Christina said.

The man beside Mr. Kingsley looked at her sharply. "Angelbloom!" he said excitedly. "Where? Do you have some?"

"This is Mr. Grady from the Chemco Pharmaceutical Company," Mr. Kingsley introduced the man. "Chemco is interested in purchasing the land where you found the angelbloom, Ashley."

"You're selling the woods? The bridge?" Christina

gasped. "No, you can't. Please, Mr. Kingsley. It wouldn't be good. Please, you —"

"Don't worry, Christina," Mr. Kingsley said with a smile. "We're not going to."

"Why don't you reconsider?" Mr. Grady asked Mr. Kingsley. "You'll never get an offer like this again. That woods isn't worth half the money we're offering. Land values around here aren't that high. But Chemco is willing to pay it to get the angelbloom." He laughed a false, high laugh. "It's certainly still cheaper than searching Tibet for it."

"I imagine it is," Mrs. Kingsley said. "Are you sure you'd have to bulldoze the woods? Isn't there any other way?"

"We wouldn't bulldoze the entire woods, just a path large enough to get trucks through." Mr. Grady turned to Christina. "You say there's a bridge out there? Could a truck get over it?"

"No. It's just an old covered bridge," Christina replied emphatically. "Very old. It barely holds people."

"Then that would probably have to go, too," he said.

"We sure could use that money," Mrs. Kingsley said.

Ashley clasped her mother's arm. "Mom, it would ruin the woods. And you can't count on the angelbloom being there. It doesn't always bloom."

"What?" Mr. Grady said. "What do you mean?"

"It's too wild and mysterious to be tamed," Ashley said. "Some things are like that."

"You don't think it can be harvested?" he asked.

"I doubt it," Ashley said.

"Mind if I send a team out tomorrow to look at the

stuff anyway?" Mr. Grady asked Mr. and Mrs. Kingsley.

"I suppose that would be all right," Mr. Kingsley agreed.

Ashley and Christina looked at one another, wide-eyed with concern. This was terrible! Ashley realized as never before how deeply she valued the bridge and the ancient woods around it. The thought of its destruction hit her like a physical pain. It just couldn't happen.

But it would happen if Mr. Grady persuaded her parents to change their minds.

18

The next day, Christina and Ashley sat on the front porch of Ashley's house, waiting. Mr. Grady's team of three men and a woman had gone into the woods in search of the angelbloom.

Champ sat with them, watching, as Christina laid her cards out on the wooden porch floor, one by one. "This is awesome," she said, studying the cards. "I'm getting the same reading I got yesterday, only slightly different. I wonder if something changed between yesterday and today."

Ashley took her eyes away from the woods and glanced down at the Native American medicine cards beside her. Each card depicted a different animal. She stared back at the woods. "They'll never find it," she murmured hopefully, thinking of the angelbloom "Not with the directions I gave them."

"You gave them bad directions?" Christina asked, smiling.

"Totally."

"Good," Christina said. "What are we going to do if they bulldoze the woods, Ashley? I can't stand the thought."

"Me, neither," Ashley agreed. If they did, it would all be her fault, too.

Christina went back to her cards. "This reading is about power and how to use it in a balanced way," she decided. "That's what this horse card here on top represents."

"That hummingbird is cute. What does he mean?" Ashley asked.

"He's joy and balance." Christina pointed to another card. "The otter here is about joy, too. What good is power and stuff if you don't enjoy your life? I think that's what they mean for this reading."

Ashley thought of the vision she'd seen inside the mist. That person who was Ashley's grown-up self hadn't enjoyed her life very much. She'd been miserable.

"These enjoyment cards are the two that are different," Christina told her. "Somehow something's gotten better for you between yesterday and today."

Ashley nodded. Something *had* improved. Inside, she knew that she wouldn't have that awful future she'd seen in the mist. She was going to have a better one, happier and more meaningful.

"See this one?" Christina tapped a card with a brown bear on its face. "The bear goes into its cave and looks for answers. You've seemed far away lately. But now you're more yourself again. Like you've returned, somehow. I think you've been deep inside yourself looking for answers."

"I think so, too," Ashley agreed. She jumped to her feet. The pharmaceutical team was coming around the stable. Ashley squinted into the sun, trying to read their expressions, but she couldn't.

Christina stood up beside her. Together, with Champ alongside, they ran to meet the team. Mr. and Mrs. Kingsley came out of the stable at the same time. They all met in the middle of the dirt road.

The team leader, a lanky man wearing glasses, took off his floppy fisherman's cap and wiped his sweaty brow. The others looked hot and exhausted, too. They didn't appear to have any angelbloom with them.

"That bridge can be very hard to find," Ashley said, talking fast to cover her nervousness. Did they realize she'd misdirected them? "I tried to give you good directions, but a woods isn't a street with signs and all, so it was sort of hard to be exact when —"

"We found it," the team leader interrupted her. "It took us a while, but we found the bridge."

Ashley paled. "You did?"

She and Christina exchanged horrified glances.

The team leader nodded. "There's nothing growing there."

Christina gripped Ashley's arm tight. "There isn't?"

"Nope."

Ashley saw that her mother and father looked relieved.

"Well, that's a shame," her mother said, smiling. "I guess it wasn't meant to be."

"Maybe not. If you people ever see any again, give us a call," the team leader requested. "In the meantime, we'll dispatch a team to Tibet. Although that will be a lot more costly."

"Getting up the Himalayas can't be easy," Mr. Kingsley remarked gleefully.

"And then you have to get down again," Mrs. Kingsley put in, sounding almost giddy.

The team leader slapped a bug on his arm and nodded. "Well, thanks for letting us look," he said, then beckoned the rest of his team to follow him to the minivan they'd arrived in.

Before they were even gone, Ashley and Christina grabbed hold of one another and danced joyfully in a circle. Mr. Kingsley and Mrs. Kingsley embraced.

"I don't know why we're so happy," Mr. Kingsley said, laughing. "We just lost a ton of money."

"The woods is worth more than any amount of money," Ashley said happily.

"It is," Mrs. Kingsley agreed. "But the money would have paid for three fine college educations, among other things."

"That's okay," Ashley said. "I'm working on a science project that's going to win me a big college scholarship."

"You sound awfully confident," Mr. Kingsley noted.

"I am," Ashley said. "I've learned a lot about my subject."

"I'm happy, too," Mrs. Kingsley said. "That woods has been there all my life. The idea of it being bulldozed really unnerved me."

"Me, too," Mr. Kingsley agreed. "I don't think they would have bulldozed just a path through the woods, either. If we sold that land, they'd want to build a factory on it or something like that. I didn't want to sell, but it would have been hard to turn our backs on the money. I'm glad the choice was taken out of our hands."

"Oh, no!" Christina cried just then. A warm breeze had lifted her medicine cards from the porch and was sailing them down the steps. She and Ashley ran to gather them up.

"Does this mean my future is sailing on the wind?" Ashley asked playfully, bending to gather the cards as they slowly fluttered to the ground.

"Maybe. Who knows?" Christina laughed, picking up cards. "You know, Ashley, I have a feeling you *are* going to win that scholarship. When you were talking, the feeling hit me really strong."

"It did? Good," Ashley said, hoping Christina's intuition would prove true once again.

"Just think," Christina said, still gathering cards, "if you worked hard maybe you could even skip a grade and go to college early, since you'd already have most of the money for it."

"Naw," Ashley disagreed.

"Why not?"

"From now on, I'm going to be very careful about rushing anything. I'll let things happen when they're supposed to."

"That sounds right," Christina agreed. "It really does." As she spoke, a second breeze lifted the remaining cards. One circled high in the air and landed facedown right on Ashley's boot.

Christina leaped over to Ashley's foot and put her hand on the card. "This is a sign," she said. "This card came right to you."

Ashley wanted to take it lightly, but she felt her pulse quicken slightly as Christina turned the card over. "What is it?"

Christina stared at the card and slowly a smile formed on her lips. She turned the card toward Ashley, revealing a soaring eagle. "The great spirit card. It's watching over you."

"Good," Ashley said, taking the card from her. "That's very good." Together they picked up the rest of the cards.

As she worked, Ashley noticed her father leading Bridey out of the stable. The foal was walking along beside her. "Ashley," her father called. "We need a name for this little gal."

"Bloomingtime," Ashley answered as the name leaped suddenly into her mind.

Her father nodded. "Okay."

"Good name," Christina said. A thoughtful look came over her. "I wonder if the angelbloom will ever come back again."

"I bet it will," Ashley said, sure that the next time they needed it, the flower would be swaying proudly on strong stems by the bridge. Standing patiently, like a blessing waiting to be received.